Andy Shepherd

THE BOY WHO FLEW WITH DRAGONS

Illustrated by Sara Ogilvie

Piccadilly
PRESS

First published in Great Britain in 2019 by
PICCADILLY PRESS
80–81 Wimpole St, London W1G 9RE
www.piccadillypress.co.uk

ISBN: 978-1-84812-735-7
also available as an ebook

1

Printed and bound by Clays Ltd, Elcograf S.p.A

Piccadilly Press is an imprint of Bonnier Zaffre Ltd,
part of Bonnier Books UK
www.bonnierbooks.co.uk

For Ian, Ben and Jonas
With all my love always

We grow dragons. Dragons that flicker, that frost, and some that fill the sky with fire.

We sit cross-legged round our dragon-fruit tree, watching and waiting. Dragons perch on our shoulders, their tails curled around our necks. Diamond eyes glitter. Claws tread. Sparks crackle. And hot smoky breath warms us to our hearts. All of us are waiting for the moment when the red ripe dragon fruit starts to glow. When it drops from the vivid tendril. When a new tiny dragon is ready to hatch. All of us are wondering what kind of dragon it will be.

Will it glow and glimmer like Flicker, shimmering through every colour from ruby red to turquoise? Will it cover us in icicles like Crystal does, leaving us to tinkle like a frozen xylophone? Will it disappear before our eyes, a master of camouflage like Dodger, or pulse with golden light as Sunny does?

Who knows? Maybe it will do all this and more. But one thing's for sure – hearing this, I bet you want one too, right? A dragon of your own. Of course you do.

But first there's something I need to tell you.

So keep listening, because you haven't heard the whole story yet. And once you have, you might not be quite so quick to rush out and grow yourself a dragon.

Because it's not just the mess, the flames, the claw marks, the smouldering sparks. It's not even the pyrotechnic poo. It's something even more devastating.

One day you will have to let your dragon go – and that, my friends, is the hardest thing of all.

1
Starlight Flicker Bright

The first thing I noticed was that Flicker wasn't there. The comforting glow of his little body had gone. I'd fallen asleep with him nestled against me as always, but I woke up with a shiver, missing his warming breath across my chest.

I rubbed my eyes, blinking the sleep away, reliving the dream I'd been having – a familiar dream that if I'd been a cat would have left me purring. Snatches of it glittered before me. Green light across the sky. A vast mountain. A rocky land below. And then it was gone.

Sitting up in bed, I saw Flicker. He was perched on the windowsill of my bedroom and it was so bright with stars and moonlight that it almost looked like morning had come. I clambered out of bed and pulled the curtains all the way back, feeling the rush of cold night air from the open window. Flicker fluttered out onto the ledge and lifted his head. He sent out a spray of sparks that fizzled in the air. They left the trace of a ring, like the fiery after-glow from a sparkler on Bonfire Night. And glittering inside the ring was the North Star. It wasn't the first time I'd found Flicker staring out of the window but it was happening more often. I watched the glow fade, then reached out and touched his back. A ripple of gold shimmered under my fingers as his scales changed colour.

I stared out of the window and pictured Ted, Kat and Kai curled up with their dragons. And I couldn't help smiling. Together we were the superhero squad and there wasn't much we couldn't do with dragons by our side.

And then Liam, our nemesis, muscled his way into the picture and stomped all over it, messing it right up, reminding me that things might not be quite that simple.

You see at the beginning of the summer he had sneaked into Grandad's garden and got himself a dragon. I know, sneaky or what! Not only that, but when his dragon breathed on stuff it made things grow really fast – and really big! After super-sizing his sunflower to try to win the school competition, Liam had quickly moved on to super-sizing a dragon fruit. The dragon that hatched out of the giant fruit went from turkey to *Tyrannosaurus* in about ten minutes.

That was definitely one you wouldn't want to curl up with! Thanks to Flicker lighting up like a beacon, Tyrannodragon had been led up into the sky and towards what we hoped was home. Although where home was for the dragons we still had no idea.

Wondering how we were going to find that out was just one of the things constantly swimming laps round my head – along with trying to guess what Liam might get up to next with the dragon he still had. The one that could make pumpkins grow to the size of Cinderella's carriage.

I was about to lean over and close the window when the bedroom door creaked open. I grabbed the curtain and yanked it across, hoping Flicker would stay behind it and out of sight. I was on constant red alert for Mum or Dad – especially these days. Mum is always juggling vet work, stray animals and my sister Lolli, like an octopus with serious circus skills, and Dad is usually locked inside his headphones-bubble of music. But even they had started to notice things. There are only so many scorch marks and claw scratches it's possible to hide. Or blame on your cat.

A little messy head appeared and I sighed with relief.

'What are you doing, Lolli?' I whispered. 'You should be asleep. Big day tomorrow.'

Lolli grinned. 'Me up now.'

I glanced at the clock next to my bed. It was three o'clock in the morning. Officially it was her birthday, but I doubted Mum and Dad would appreciate starting the celebration this early. I shook my head.

'Not time yet, Lollibob. Much too early.'

She rumpled her face into a frown. But it quickly vanished when the curtain started bulging and Flicker found his way out through the gap.

He zipped over and started circling her head, letting out little smoky puffs. She giggled, delighted, eyes twinkling as brightly as Grandad's did. I couldn't help grinning. Especially when I thought of my secret. You see, ever since she'd tried to hatch a dragon from a pineapple and turned our lounge into a swamp in the process, I'd known that more than anything Lolli wanted a dragon. And so with the latest crop of dragon fruits red and ripe, I knew I could give her the best birthday present ever.

It was time for Lolli to have a dragon of her own.

2
The Blue Tornado and the Not-So-Early Worm

Lolli made it to five o'clock before she declared her birthday officially open. Dressed in her Batman costume she paraded up and down the hall banging a drum until the rest of us stumbled out to join the festivities.

When we got to Nana and Grandad's later for Birthday Breakfast, Lolli burst through the door like a miniature tornado. She was entirely fuelled by icing, after licking out the bowl Mum had been using to decorate her cake. Mum had made a mermaid on top of a rock – well, that was its official title. To be fair, it looked more like a seal in a wig. And that was if you squinted and were feeling generous.

Nana put down the stack of pancakes she'd been holding and caught Lolli up in a huge hug.

'Hippity hoppity happity birthday, little Lolli,' she chuckled.

Lollibob squeezed Nana tight and giggled happily.

'Guppie!' she cried, and started looking around for Grandad. I peered out the window, expecting him to be coming up the garden. It would be just like him to be out digging at this time of the day.

And then I saw a little look pass between Mum and Nana.

'Grandad's having a lie-in,' Nana said, lowering Lolli to the floor.

Now to most people this might not seem like that big a deal, and Mum would probably sell the house for a lie-in. But not Grandad. He'd go and embarrass the early worm by being up, dressed and mowing the lawn before it had even wriggled out of bed.

'Hey up, Chipstick,' Grandad said with a grin as I gingerly opened the bedroom door. He was sitting up in bed with a tray on his lap, building a boat out of a massive pile of matchsticks. He lowered it to safety as Lolli twirled her way into the room and leaped onto the bed.

'Are you OK, Grandad?' I asked, perching on the edge of the mattress.

'I'm fine. Nana's just being a fusspot, that's all.'

Lolli wriggled in closer, and Grandad tucked her under his arm.

'So you can still come to the party?' I asked.

Grandad gave Lolli a squeeze. 'Not this time,' he said.

And I could tell he was just as disappointed about it as we were, but in true Grandad fashion he wasn't about to say that.

'But you'll save me some jelly, won't you, Lolli?' He grinned.

Lolli was giving him a hard stare and I wondered if she might go supersonic. It really wasn't a good idea to mess with the party plan. But instead she leaned over and kissed Grandad on his whiskery cheek. Then she reached into her pocket and took out a sticky lump of blue icing. It was covered in fluff from her pocket, but Grandad obviously knew this was an offering of epic proportions.

'Thank you, Lolli,' he said gravely. 'It's just what I need to liven up that there porridge. Can you pop it in the bowl for me?'

Lolli climbed out of bed and happily began stirring the dish of cold gloop which had been Grandad's breakfast and was now a murky shade of blue.

'So, Chipstick . . .' Grandad said.

And I knew exactly what he meant by that *and* what was coming next. You see, in the chaos of Liam hatching his super-sized dragon, Grandad had found out all about us keeping Flicker and the others. And even though it was brilliant that Grandad knew now and I didn't have to fib any more, what wasn't so brilliant was that he'd insisted I made a deal. And the deal was that we'd let all the dragons go at the end of the summer holidays.

We'd seen what a properly big dragon could do, the havoc it could cause, and Grandad said having four that size was not something any of us could handle.

A tiny part of me knew he was right. But it was such a tiny part it was easy to squish it flat and sit on it. The thing was, I still hadn't told the others what I'd agreed to. I just couldn't bear to break it to them. I knew how disappointed they'd be.

I kept hoping I could change Grandad's mind. And I did, a bit, buying us two extra months. He'd finally agreed to let us keep them until October, until Ted, me and last of all Lolli had had our birthdays. But I knew there would be no more persuading him. And with Lolli's party hours away, time was running out.

'After today it's time to let the dragons go. We had a deal, remember?' Grandad whispered.

My hands started feeling prickly. I really didn't want to answer him, because if I did I'd be agreeing to it all over again. And the more time I'd had to think about it, the more I'd realised it just wasn't something I *could* agree to. I needed a different plan. But I couldn't think of anything. Nothing at all. Here was I with a brain that usually couldn't stop flinging out ideas and it was like it had decided to switch off.

And then Nana and Mum clattered into the room and started fussing round, tidying things up and telling us to let Grandad have a bit of 'peace and quiet'.

He was looking me square in the eye and I could pretty much see the words he wasn't saying lit up above his head: 'Remember what you promised.'

I let Nana bundle me out of the room, the hot prickly feeling spreading fast. Because, even though I'd known exactly what Grandad had been thinking, I couldn't nod. I couldn't even really look him in the eye any more. Because I already knew I wasn't going to be able to keep my promise.

3
A Present
for Lolli

Look, before you get all judgy, I couldn't possibly let
the dragons go now. How could I? Not when Lolli was
just about to hatch one. Here you go, Lollibob, your
dream's come true and by the way you have to give it
back tomorrow. Honestly, how mean would that be?

Leaving Mum and Nana fussing over Grandad,
and Dad listening to the radio, I led Lolli out into the
garden.

I could see Grim – that's Grandad's grumpy
neighbour – over the fence. He was loading a
wheelbarrow with beanstalks he'd just pulled out. I

didn't want to run into him and burst Lolli's birthday bubble. Grim still hadn't got over the utter devastation to his garden that Liam's super-sized dragon had caused.

Of course, thanks to Grandad, Grim believed it was a methane explosion caused by his compost bins – not a gigantic fiery fart from a ginormous dragon. But even with the compost-bin explanation, he still seemed to blame me. At least that's what it felt like from the permanent scowl he aimed at me whenever he saw me. I stopped by the beehives, which Grandad had promised to fill with bees one day, and lifted the lid off one to show Lolli. She stuck her head inside eagerly, and then popped it out again looking disappointed. I think she thought I'd put her birthday present in there.

Thankfully Grim was marching his way past us up to his house. I kept my back turned to him and pretended to be very interested in the hive until he'd disappeared inside.

Then I headed further down the garden, leading the still-disgruntled Lolli by the hand. Flicker fluttered above us until we reached the dragon-fruit tree. Then he flew down and landed on one of the long cactus-like leaves. Dragon-fruit trees are about the weirdest-looking plants you'll ever see. Grandad said he thought it looked like an upturned mophead when we cleared the garden and saw it for the first time. A spiky green mop anyway. It also has vivid yellow and orange tendrils and special moon-white flowers that bloom for just one night. And after the flowers have bloomed, that's when the dragon fruits start to grow.

Lolli peered at the tree, but she knew better than to touch. I'd always been super-strict about that. The fruits needed time to grow and ripen, and I couldn't risk little hands pulling them off before they were ready. But today was different.

I could see a few dragon fruits on the tree and they were all a rich red. In fact, some of them looked fit to burst, with their spiky pineapple-like leaves bulging out. It was so good to see the dragon-fruit tree looking healthy again. With no more super-sizing dragon breath to deal with, and a daily sprinkling of ash, it was going from strength to strength.

'Hey, Lolli,' I said trying to keep things calm. I figured when I told her today was the day she'd get to hatch her very own dragon, the scream she'd unleash might just break the sound barrier.

'Can I hear your most whisperiest, quietest voice?'

Lolli screwed up her nose and mouth in a puzzled look.

I whispered the question again, almost mouthing the words and giving her a smile to show it was the start of a game. Lolli could never resist a game.

'Shhh,' she breathed as quietly as she could and started crouching down to match the size of her teeny-tiny voice.

'Brilliant,' I whispered back. 'Now, can you use that voice when I show you your birthday present?'

Lolli's eyes went wide. She nodded seriously.

'Good,' I said. I took her hand and led her closer to the tree.

I grinned. 'Happy birthday, Lolli!'

She looked from me to the tree and back again.
I nodded towards one of the fruits. 'You do want a
dragon?' I said, teasing. 'I mean if you've gone off the
idea, that's fine.' To be honest I had had some second,
third and fourth thoughts about her having a dragon.
But in the end I'd decided that between us, Flicker and
I could handle things.

Her eyes nearly popped out on
stalks and I could feel her hand
jiggling in mine as she realised
what I was saying. I felt the
jiggly feeling shoot all the way
up my arm too and I couldn't help
grinning.

Eagerly, Lolli stepped
forward and reached up
towards one of the fruits.
Flicker puffed a smoky
breath in her face and

she gave a little sneeze and pulled her hand back. She tried again with another fruit and Flicker did the same. She lowered her hand, a frown on her face. Slowly she moved around the tree, carefully inspecting each of the fruits. Finally she spotted one deep within the leaves of the tree. It was tiny compared to the rest, but when she reached towards it, the red skin of the fruit began to glow. And the next second it dropped into Lolli's outstretched hands.

She stared at it, her mouth in a little round 'O'.

Then with a POP the fruit burst and a dragon shot out. It landed on the ground in a sticky mess of seeds and pulp. I watched Lolli bend down and gently scoop the little dragon up. I couldn't help remembering the night Flicker had burst out of his fruit. And how it had felt when he had hopped onto my hand for the very first time.

This dragon was brilliant silver with bright blue spines along its back and at the end of its tail. Its horns shone like they had been dipped in the sparkly glitter glue Lolli covered all her pictures in.

And then it did something unexpected – something none of the other dragons had ever done. It opened its mouth and, instead of sparks, it started singing. I don't mean singing with words. It was just making this sound. That I can't even describe. Except that I got this jumble of pictures in my mind when I heard it.

I saw the moon reflected in a rippling river. And those green lights you see over the North Pole. And the colour of the sky before there's a storm. And it was like all those things made sounds and they'd swirled round together to make this one amazing sound. And this happy feeling spread through me like drinking hot chocolate on a cold day. It was sort of like that.

Lolli looked as spellbound as I felt.

One thing was for sure – I'd just won the prize for best birthday present *ever*.

4

Once Upon a Fairy-Tale Party

Lolli was having a party in the village hall with a bouncy castle. I have no clue why Mum had to invite the whole of Lolli's nursery. I could have told her three three-year-olds was more than enough, let alone thirty-three. Add to that four excitable dragons and you can imagine how things went.

It all started with Lolli's grand entrance. Mum had decided it was going to be a Princesses and Knights party. So everything was covered in pictures of pink frilly princesses and cartoon knights.

Most of the girls were wearing fancy dresses they

kept tripping over. And the boys were covered in tin-foil armour. But some had decided they wanted the best of both worlds, so there were princesses with cardboard swords and several knights in tutus.

And then there was Lolli. She had other ideas for her costume.

And I bet you can guess what?

With a lot of help from me and Nana, Lolli roared her way into the village hall as a fire-breathing dragon. Of course the silver paint hadn't quite covered the cereal boxes, and several of the cardboard spines had already fallen off, but that didn't stop Lolli. She burst

into the crowd of startled princesses and knights, scattering them in all directions.

Mum and Dad disappeared into the little kitchen, leaving me to 'sort out some games'. The food was already laid out on tables at the end of the hall, so I'm pretty sure they were just hiding in there. Not that I could blame them. Luckily for me though, I wasn't alone. There aren't many best mates who would stick by you in the face of a three-year-old's birthday party – but Ted, Kat and Kai had agreed to come and help and they didn't let me down. It's exactly that kind of thing that makes us the superhero squad.

'I think this lot need entertaining,' Kat shouted over the noise of yelling princesses. 'What games have you got organised?'

I shrugged. 'I think Mum made a Pass the Parcel.'

'Is that it?' Kat shrieked. 'You need more than that to keep this lot busy.'

'I think she thought the bouncy castle would do the job,' I said.

We all turned and looked at the miniature wobbly castle. It was only big enough for about three kids and the tower part was already sagging. It had looked a lot bigger and a lot cooler in the picture.

'You know what I think?' Kat said. 'I think this fairy-tale party needs some real live dragons!'

We all looked at each other and grinned.

Ted quickly set up camp at one end of the hall. He'd tucked Sunny into his jacket and pulled the collar right up. Cupping his hands round his mouth and shielding the little dragon's head at the same time, he started breathing fire. Or that's what it looked like to the little group of open-mouthed kids who soon gathered around him.

Meanwhile, instead of balloon animals, Kat produced ice creatures made by Crystal, who was hiding underneath one of the tables. The children giggled delightedly as she reached under the flaps of the tablecloth and pulled out a tiny sparkly dog that looked just like Dexter, Kat and Kai's terrier pup.

'Come see MagiKai, the masterful magician,' Kai hollered. 'I shall make a dragon appear before your very eyes.'

He held up a seemingly empty bag for them all to peer into. Muttering a few words he waved his arm across it and suddenly Dodger appeared. He'd been the same blue as the bag, in order to hide, then changed to a bright orange colour so he would stand out.

There were gasps and squeals and then they all clapped and shouted for him to do it again.

Not wanting to miss out on the fun, I decided to join in with Flicker. I'd seen how much Lolli loved chasing bubbles round the garden. So, hidden up my sleeve, his little head peeking out, Flicker started making smoke rings for the rest of the kids to chase. I have to admit we were doing a pretty good job. And no one was attacking each other any more.

Then the door opened and a boy with a mop of black hair appeared with what looked like a giant frilly pom-pom stuck to his leg. Lolli squealed and raced over to the pom-pom, which unstuck itself from the boy. It turned out to be another princess, who had arrived fashionably late. This princess was related to our arch-nemesis, Liam Sawston.

Liam's got an older brother and a younger sister. His brother Jay is probably the coolest person you will ever meet. He oozes cool. He stood there with cool flicky hair, wearing a cool leather jacket, cool jeans, cool sunglasses and a cool T-shirt that had Darth Vader's head on it. And he just said: 'Hi.'

See what I mean? Cool.

Liam's sister Bea is as cute as Jay is cool. She is one of those little kids that makes grown-ups stop what they're doing and go, 'Awwwwwwwwwwwww.' And Lolli and Bea have been best buddies since they started nursery. The same nursery that Liam and me used to go to. And where, according to Mum, Liam and me were best of friends. Which of course is totally crazy.

I can't help wondering if Lolli and Bea will still be friends when they're ten. Or if they'll turn into deadliest enemies like Liam and me are now.

'Look out, King of Trouble's here,' Kai said nodding towards a figure lurking behind Jay. And there he was. Liam. The one Sawston who was definitely *not* cool *or* cute.

'What's *he* doing here?' Ted asked.

'Looking for trouble, I bet,' I said. Liam and his super-sizing dragon were the last thing we needed.

But before we could do anything about him there came a scream of epic proportions.

5
Flying Dragons, Screaming Lions and the King of Trouble

I spun round and saw Kai in a tug of war. A grubby knight had grabbed the bag with Dodger in and was shoving his arm in for a good rootle around.

But that wasn't the half of it. Sunny had got bored of being stuck in Ted's jacket and had wriggled free and found the party food – *and* the chocolate fountain. He was utterly covered in the stuff and dripping it onto the heads below as he soared around the hall.

Luckily, a dollop of chocolate unexpectedly splatted on the knight's face and he yanked his hand out of the bag to wipe it away – just in time too, as a blast from Dodger set light to it.

Without a backwards glance, the knight sped off to join the rest of the children as they chased around with open mouths, trying to catch mouthfuls of the sticky sweetness.

But everyone started slipping on the melting ice animals and soon the hall was full of a crying tangle of frills and tin foil. Sunny veered round and flapped his way back to the table of food, ready to dive into the chocolate fountain once more.

Unaware of his lucky escape earlier, the grubby chocolate-coated knight spotted Dodger taking refuge in the stack of Lolli's presents piled up next to the table. He raced over and started ripping his way through them in a desperate search to find the dragon. Alarmed, Dodger shot out from behind one of the boxes. With a battle cry the knight dived at the little shape . . . and landed flailing and wailing with a crash on one end of the table of food. And as the other end tipped up, a chocolate-splattered Sunny launched from the fountain. But his wings were weighed down by the setting chocolate and he was sent spinning across the plates of food until he landed slap bang on Lolli's birthday cake. The mermaid seal was squished under the dragon, and I turned just in time to see Lolli's face crumple.

She fled from the room as princesses, knights and dragons tore around in chaos.

'What are we going to do?' cried Kai.

'If Mum and Dad come back in now we're really in trouble,' I yelled back.

'You mean more trouble than a room full of three-year-olds covered in chocolate who've just seen flying dragons?' Kat replied.

Suddenly there was a high-pitched squeak, like someone was letting the air out of a balloon. The bouncy castle collapsed in on itself as Crystal landed on it and her claws sank into the saggy tower.

'Kat, can you keep my mum and dad out of here?' I cried. 'Ted and Kai, I need you to try to calm things down a bit. Do a game of Sleeping Lions or something. Just stop –' I waved my hand at the chaos – 'this.'

Leaving them to it, I hurried out of the hall. I had to find Lolli.

She wasn't in the corridor and I could see Kat hadn't found her in the kitchen with Mum and Dad. I swung the door to the girls' toilet open and called out. But no one answered. Pressing my nose against the glass of the double doors, I peered outside. And then scowled. Liam, bent over the bike rack, was spinning round and round on the bar in a whirl of somersaults. I was willing to bet he was just waiting to sneak in and cause even more trouble.

Suddenly I heard a giggle. I pushed the door open and there, just outside, was a little heap of boxes.

'Lolli,' I whispered with relief.

Liam stopped spinning and pulled himself upright. I glared at him.

'Come on, Lolli,' I said.

Lolli shook her head. 'Spindy spindy,' she gabbled, pointing at Liam.

'Come on,' I cajoled. 'Time to eat some of that lovely food. The cake still tastes good even if it's a bit flat. Promise.'

She held out a sticky hand towards Liam as if she was inviting him to come too.

Liam looked awkward and I half expected him to laugh in her face. He didn't though; he just looked at me for a second. I stared back. I don't know what he was looking at me for. It wasn't like I was about to invite him in. He turned to Lolli and shook his head. Thank goodness for that. Admittedly it looked as if he might have stopped Lolli wandering off, but let's face it, the last thing this party needed was Liam 'King of Trouble' Sawston. Things were bad enough already.

Lolli didn't budge and kept her hand outstretched.

'Go on,' Liam muttered sulkily. 'Or you'll miss all the fun.'

Lolli looked at me as if I could make a difference.

I shrugged. 'Another time,' I lied.

She wiped her hand across her nose, gave Liam a smile and skipped back inside. Only Lolli could want Liam Sawston at her birthday party.

Judging by the screaming, crying, food throwing and fighting, Kai and Ted hadn't been that successful at the whole calming-down thing. It was more like Screaming Lions than Sleeping Lions. I looked around for Flicker and saw him being chased by a parade of princesses.

Lolli reached into the main box she was wearing as the dragon's body. She pulled her hand out and I saw she was holding the tiny silver dragon. She lifted the dragon up to her face and stroked its head.

'Tinkle, sing lullybies,' she said.

And suddenly the silver dragon began to sing. The strange sound filled the hall and it was like watching the Pied Piper of Hamelin in that old story. Children who had been running full pelt stopped on the spot, and the ones who were flinging cake let their arms drop. The dragons paused in their frenzied escape. Everyone just calmed down. Even I could feel my hammering heart start to slow.

'*Tinkle, Tinkle, 'ickle dar,*' Lolli sang happily.

It looked like Tinkle, the singing silver dragon, had just saved Lolli's party.

6
You Did WHAT?

It's a good job no one really listens to three-year-olds. We watched all the mums and dads smiling and nodding and totally ignoring the clamour of thirty-three little children chattering on about all the dragons they'd seen zooming around the hall.

It was like Grandad said. No one actually wanted to believe in dragons, so even if the grown-ups *had* seen Flicker or the others with their own eyes they'd have come up with some other explanation for it.

Now, that's not to say you shouldn't do your best to keep your dragon secret. Don't go getting all relaxed about it and thinking you don't need to be careful. Because there'll always be someone who'll find out. Like Liam did, creeping around and spying on us. And believe me, you don't want to be dealing with someone like him.

When Liam first got his dragon, we'd all been worried that he would blab about it, unable to resist showing off. It was why we'd tried to catch his dragon so we could let it go before he gave the game away.

But in the end he hadn't told anyone. And actually he'd been keeping a low profile since hatching the ginormous dragon. Just as well too, since he'd scarpered and left us to sort out his mess, which we weren't going to forget in a hurry! Seeing him at Lolli's party though reminded us all that he was out there. Waiting.

On the way home we spotted him again, hanging about by the swings and roundabout. I wondered if he'd been planning an ambush. But if that was it he'd picked the worst place to hide ever. We'd practically have to step over him to get by. And he was doing a rubbish job as lookout, hunkered down, stabbing at the ground with a stick.

There was no sign of his dragon, or anyone else for that matter. No doubt he'd scared all the little kids away.

We all eyed him warily as we passed, just in case he had some trick up his sleeve. But he barely glanced up.

'You know I'm starting to wonder about his dragon,' Kat whispered.

'What do you mean?' I asked.

'Well, at the start of the holidays we were always seeing giant flowers spilling out of window boxes and people disappearing into their huge garden hedges. But lately things have been pretty normal-sized. Don't you think?'

Now she mentioned it, I had to admit she was right. There was a time when just walking down a street you could end up fighting your way through a tangle of low-hanging branches from some tree Liam's dragon had blasted, but that wasn't happening now.

'Maybe he's found a way to keep it under control,' Ted suggested.

Kat didn't look convinced. The way Liam acted around his dragon, I agreed with her. He'd been so busy figuring out how he could use the dragon to wreak havoc, I doubted he'd have much interest in learning about what it liked – or in training it.

'Maybe he's got it locked away somewhere so it doesn't cause him any trouble,' said Kai.

Kat looked horrified. 'Do you really think he'd do that?' She looked from Kai to me. 'What if he's hurt it?' she squeaked.

I couldn't believe even Liam would sink that low, but what if he had?

'I think we should put the plan back into action,' she said. 'We need to find his dragon, make sure it's OK and actually catch it this time. And then we have to let it go.'

The others nodded fiercely.

But I just sat there. I had started to feel sick. And it wasn't the biscuits, cake, fizzy orange and handfuls of jellybeans I'd stuffed myself with. It was hearing those words: *'let it go'*.

The party was over. Not just Lolli's but the whole summer party we'd been having with the dragons.

'What's up with you, Tomas?' Kai asked. 'You've gone greener than Dodger hiding out in Dad's lettuces.'

I looked around at them. I couldn't leave it any longer, however much I wanted to ignore it. It was time to tell them about the deal I'd made with Grandad.

'YOU DID *WHAT*?' yelled Kai. 'I can't believe you did that. You *can't* do that. *I'm* not doing it. No way. Nope. Just no.'

Ted had paused in the middle of feeding Sunny popcorn and was staring at me. Sunny bypassed Ted's frozen hand and stuck his head straight into the open bag. But Ted didn't seem to notice.

Only Kat was looking at me without laser beams shooting out of her eyes. She turned to Crystal with a thoughtful look on her face.

'You knew about this all summer and didn't say anything?' Ted said at last.

I nodded. 'I didn't know how to tell you,' I said lamely. 'I knew it would spoil the summer holidays. Look, I don't want to let Flicker go either. That's the last thing I want.'

The laser beams dimmed a little.

'So we're not actually going to do it then?' said Ted.

I shrugged. 'I've managed to persuade Grandad to let us keep them this long. But this time he's not going to change his mind.'

'Then we just won't tell him,' Kai said.

I pictured Grandad the first time he'd seen the dragons. The wink he'd given me. And how good it felt not to lie to him any more. I hated the idea of going back to that squirmy uncomfortable feeling I got whenever I kept something from him. Like wriggly squiggly worms were holding the finals of the World Knot-Tying Championship in my tummy.

But what could I do? I couldn't let the superhero squad down and I *definitely* didn't want to lose Flicker.

7
The Elephant in the Bobble Hat

I spent all that night worrying about what I would do when I next saw Grandad. I still needed to go over every day and sprinkle ash on the tree. It would feel horrible lying to him when he was poorly. But I couldn't just avoid him. That would be even worse, especially when he was stuck in bed.

And then something awful happened that meant I didn't have to worry about lying to Grandad. But I did have a whole *new* thing to worry about.

I knew something was wrong when Mum came into my bedroom and didn't make any comments about the carpet of clothes, the empty packets from our super-snacktastic post-party picnic or the scorch mark I'd failed to hide under my desk. And when she held up the packet of chocolate biscuits I knew something was very, *very* wrong indeed.

She held the packet out to me and I took it nervously. She motioned for me to take one.

As I bit into it, she smiled. But it was one of those droopy smiles that hardly makes it past the corners of the person's mouth, never mind all the way up to their eyes.

'Now I don't want you to worry, Tomas,' she began.

Which has to be the worst possible thing you can say to someone, right? I mean, if I wasn't worrying before, then of course I'm going to when someone tells me not to. That's just normal. Only my brain went into mega-overdrive and started thinking up my absolute worst worry.

'It's all fine,' she went on. 'It's just Grandad.'

Hello? Now my worry swelled up as fast as Liam's super-size dragon. It was positively planet-sized.

'He's had an accident,' she said.

And the planet exploded right there and then into a thousand million billion pieces.

In the end I learned a valuable lesson. Having my imagination is great – most of the time. But sometimes, just sometimes, it can land me in a whole heap of unnecessary mess.

Because what had happened wasn't good – but it wasn't the completely absolutely worst worry after all.

Grandad had got fed up of being stuck in bed and eating boring porridge and had sneaked out to get himself one of Nana's jammy tarts. But while he was balancing on the little stool and reaching up to Nana's 'not at all secret' secret stash of goodies, he'd fallen. And broken his hip.

What it did mean was Grandad would be in hospital for a little while. And because Lolli had been a tiny bit sick in the night the nurses had told Mum and Dad not to bring us in. I reckon it had more to do with all the blue icing than a bug, but I wasn't going to say that. If I'm honest I was a little bit relieved that I wouldn't have to lie to Grandad's face. I knew the first thing he'd ask about was whether we'd let the dragons go yet.

Over the next few days the superhero squad all tried to carry on as usual but it was difficult. The threat of Grandad's deal sort of hung over us. You know that phrase 'the elephant in the room'? It means when there's something really big that everyone knows but no one is talking about. Well, the elephant just got bigger and bigger and bigger. Until he was taking up most of the room and we all felt a bit squashed whenever we met up.

'Let's plan what we're going to do for Halloween,' Ted suggested after school, neatly elbowing the elephant out the way. Everyone nodded except me. I was distracted by the elephant, who was now sulking and blowing huge raspberries at us with his trunk. You can see the problems caused by my over-active imagination – now I was feeling sorry that someone had upset an imaginary elephant, who by the way had taken up wearing a bobble hat.

'Yeah, come on,' Kat said. 'I've already got my costume sorted. Thanks to Crystal's ice-tastic powers I'm going as Icicle Girl. My new superhero alter ego.'

'And I'm going as the amazing Telekinesis,' said Kai. He held his hands up to his head and screwed up his face in what I guessed was meant to be a look of intense concentration. It actually looked like he'd just sat on a nail. A towel lifted off the ground and flew across the room, carried by a suitably disguised Dodger. The effect was pretty cool.

'With everyone dressed up, it's the perfect night to have a bit of fun with these guys,' Kai said.

'Awesome,' said Ted excitedly. 'I can be The Flame.' And Sunny belched fire as if in agreement.

They all looked at me. And I looked at Flicker. A superhero's superpower didn't immediately flash into my mind when I looked at him. To be honest, I'd always felt a bit like everyone else thought they'd got the cooler dragons. Which wasn't fair because Flicker had been the one who'd saved our bacon twice now. If it wasn't for his bright ideas we'd probably still have been battling Liam's super-sized dragon. It's just that Flicker wasn't as obviously flashy as the others. Flickery – but not flashy.

'I'm keeping mine a surprise,' I said lamely.

We spent the next hour drawing up our route for maximum sweet collection and planning the tricks we'd unleash if we didn't get a treat.

I had to admit it did sound great. Even the elephant was nodding. Maybe it was just what we all needed. I mean, what could possibly go wrong, right?

8
Happy Halloween, Cloud Boy

On Halloween night Lolli danced in through the door wearing her leotard, pink tutu and a witch's hat and waving a star-shaped wand. It was quite understated for her. And then she tipped a jar of glitter over herself and I realised she'd painted the leotard with glue. She definitely sparkled anyway.

While Mum bundled Lolli and Dad outside and started desparkling the carpet, I met up with Ted, Kat and Kai. Or should I say The Flame, Icicle Girl and Telekinesis. When I turned up they all went a bit quiet, like they were trying to decide what they should say.

'You're Cloud Boy?' said Kai, eyeing my grey top and trousers.

I frowned.

Kat jumped in. 'No, I get it you're . . .' She paused and tapped the grey cardboard dome on my head, then traced her fingers along the squiggly lines I'd drawn on it. 'Um . . . Rhino Boy?'

A huff exploded out of me. How could they not be getting this?

'Forget it,' I said.

Grandad always told me, 'Play to your strengths, Chipstick.' Well, I had. Flicker was full of bright ideas and actually so was I. So it had seemed like a brilliant plan to take that as my superpower.

'I was meant to be Captain Brain,' I said. 'You know, solving crimes with the power of the mind.'

'Oh . . . er . . . cool,' Ted said.

Except it wasn't really, because part of my brain had come unstuck and I was desperately trying to push it back on while I spoke. I could tell he was trying not to laugh.

'Plus,' I added, scrabbling to impress them now, 'whatever I imagine appears, and so I make whatever I want happen. I just have to imagine it. It's the ultimate superpower.'

None of them looked that convinced. Ted smirked and said: 'Don't suppose you can imagine me a giant custard doughnut by any chance? I'm starving!' The others broke out in fits of giggles.

'Oh, never mind – let's just get going,' I grumbled.

Funnily enough, as my pillowcase filled up with sweets it helped lift my mood a bit. And so did the tricks. It was pretty hysterical seeing Kai doing his mind-moving act in front of people. And you should have seen one woman's face when Ted's head seemed to set on fire, thanks to a well-timed – and thankfully well-aimed – breath by Sunny. She totally screamed.

I saw Liam being dragged along by Bea. She was dressed as a pumpkin and looked so cute that people stuffed whole handfuls of sweets into her bag. They seemed to have completely forgotten about Liam standing empty-handed next to her. Or maybe they

just didn't think much of his costume. It *was* a bit lame. He was only wearing a cloak over his school uniform, and it looked as if he'd shaved a random patch of hair from his head. Come to think of it, that might have had something to do with his dragon. It wasn't the first time we'd seen him looking the worse for wear. At least I could tell Kat he must still have the dragon. It was pretty clear though that he hadn't had much luck with training it, which meant Kai had probably been right about him keeping it locked up.

As I was about to join the others, Liam caught my eye and opened his mouth to say something. But I pretended not to notice and ran up the path to the next house. Best not to give him the chance, not with half my brain still only held on with sellotape.

After another hour of trick-or-treating Ted and Sunny were both in hyper-drive. And the fiery halo Sunny provided for Ted's costume had become increasingly explosive. Jets of flame shot out from Ted as he whooped and hollered his way down the street.

Even Crystal was going a bit loopy. Kat couldn't eat any of her sweets as Crystal kept breathing on them so it was like chewing on an ice cube.

'Oi,' Kat yelled at Kai after she'd nearly broken another tooth on a frozen marshmallow. 'Stop dropping things on me.'

'Sorry,' Kai said, shrugging. 'It's not actually me doing it, remember? Dodger's just decided to take it to the next level.'

'Yeah, well, stop him,' she shrieked as a can of lemonade swung perilously over her head, threatening to empty its contents over her.

But looking around at the increasingly manic dragons, I wasn't at all sure we were going to be able to stop them. Once again, things had rapidly got out of control.

9
Captain Brain and the Lightning Bolt

People were fleeing in panic from the fires Sunny kept setting off. And Crystal was too busy freezing everything else to help put them out. Having eaten so much sugar, the dragons were pooing more as well. Explosions started erupting along garden paths on either side. Dodger, not so helpfully, zipped back and forth dropping a cascade of lollipops and sweets. Witches, wizards, ghosts, pumpkins, superheroes and cartoon characters ran helter-skelter, trying to catch the raining treats.

Looking around, I knew it was time for Captain

Brain to step in. Here was my chance to show everyone what I could do.

'Think, Captain Brain, think,' I urged myself, banging my domed skull. 'If only I could conjure up a storm,' I muttered. 'That's what we really need.'

A downpour would put out all the fires, wash away any unexploded poo and send everyone running indoors. But how was I meant to produce one of those exactly? The most I could offer was a bunch of water pistols and a garden hose.

While I was trying to wrestle my thoughts into some kind of actual plan, Flicker wriggled his way out of my pocket and shot up into the air. I watched him flying higher and higher. His little sparks twinkled in the clear black sky like extra stars. I didn't know what he was up to, but I knew if anyone could help me, it was him.

For a second he just seemed to disappear. I kept my eyes locked on the sky, remembering the night in Grandad's garden when he had led the super-sized dragon away. He had helped us then, and I had to believe he would again.

I raised my arms and shouted after him: 'Go, Flicker! Go on! You can do it.'

Whatever 'it' was.

A cloud scudded in front of the moon and everything went dark. I squinted through the gloom, hearing the sound of the others still dashing round madly after their dragons and now crashing blindly into things and each other.

Then a whistling wind blew up out of nowhere. The moon reappeared and the sky turned a weird eerie colour as if someone had tipped orangeade over the skyline. More clouds filled the sky. Huge billowing ones that loomed low over the street. And then the rain started. Just a misty drizzle at first, but then huge fat drops that sizzled on the fires. I stared up at the sky. Hadn't I just been imagining a storm? Good grief – did I *actually* have mind powers after all? This was incredible!

Then I noticed Flicker zooming back down. He was glowing and rapidly changing colour. As he drew nearer he began circling the street, then spiralling inwards in an ever smaller loop until finally he was just spinning on the spot. Faster and faster he spun. And with every spin the rain beat down harder and the wind blew more fiercely. As he whirled around it was like watching a tornado at the eye of a storm.

And then as if a bolt of lightning had struck me –
which it hadn't luckily – I understood. This wasn't me
with mind powers. This was Flicker. A little dragon
quietly being himself and now playing to his strengths,
just as Grandad always said I should.

All this time I hadn't seen it. But now the truth
shone out as clear as the North Star.

I stood there in the pouring rain. The biggest grin
on my face. Eyes fixed on Flicker. My cloud-shaping,
lightning-crackling, weather-brewing storm dragon.

Afterwards, drenched but still grinning, I sat with
Icicle Girl, Telekinesis and The Flame. As the storm
had calmed, so did the dragons. And now they were
curled on our shoulders sleeping.

'You know what, Tomas – it looks like Flicker
has some superpowers after all. We just didn't notice,'
Ted said.

'I know,' Kai replied. 'I mean, looking back, it was there all along. Remember that night with Grim and the flaming cabbages? It suddenly started raining, out of the blue. And the same thing happened that time at the Caldwells' farm when the barn went up in flames. We thought it was just another bit of luck.'

Kai was right – it wasn't the first time Flicker had understood what was needed and come to the rescue.

'I reckon you should have a new name though, after what you and Flicker did tonight,' said Ted. 'With your ideas and his tornado twirling – how about Captain Brain-Storm?'

Kai grinned and slapped me on the back.

'Nothing you can't handle with a bit of belief, a whole lot of imagination and the power of a storm-wielding dragon behind you, hey, Tomas?'

I grinned. I could live with Captain Brain-Storm.

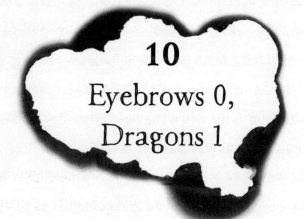

10
Eyebrows 0,
Dragons 1

Over the past months I'd found out that having a
dragon was a lot more work than looking after our cat
Tomtom – or the little family of worms in the Keep
Your Own Wormery kit I'd got for last year's birthday.
Don't think that just because you've got a handful
of terrapins or a long-haired guinea pig that you
know about pet-based chores. Because you really
don't, not on this scale. Of course Tomtom and the
worms can't fly or warm my hands with their breath,
so as far as I'm concerned Flicker's definitely worth
the extra work.

But after Halloween it wasn't just the basic looking-after and the regular chores keeping all of us busy. I couldn't help noticing everyone was looking a bit frazzled – and I mean *actually* frazzled. Ted had lost most of a sleeve to one of Sunny's belches. It was a good job he wasn't wearing the jumper at the time.

But it was only when Kat and Kai staggered into my room a couple of days later that I found out exactly how bad things had got.

Ted and I were flicking raisins, seeing whose dragon could catch most in mid-air. So far Flicker was winning forty-eight to two. Though that might have had something to do with Sunny being more interested in some hairy stale popcorn under my bed.

The first thing I noticed was how surprised Kai looked. It took me a second to work out why. And then I realised.

'Er . . . Kai, where are your eyebrows?'

His forehead wrinkled as he looked up and then down, attempting a frown. But without eyebrows he still just looked astonished.

'That'd be Dodger sneaking up on me,' he sighed.

'We need one of your woolly hats, Tomas,' Kat said. 'Before our mum notices. I mean, I thought the ones I painted on him were fine, but apparently not.'

'Yeah, well, if I wanted eyebrows that big, I'd stick caterpillars to my face,' Kai said crossly.

While I fished out some suitable headgear, everyone flopped on my bed. Ted launched into full-on fact-file mode, telling Kai that the world's longest eyebrow ever was over nineteen centimetres long.

'That's almost as long as this furry pencil case,' he said, waggling it above Kai's eyes.

I handed Kai the hat and noticed Kat watching Crystal and Dodger. The two dragons were locked in a fire and ice duel, which was in danger of scorching half my bedroom.

Flicker flew down and settled on the bed next to her. I watched his scales shimmering their familiar red as he scratched the quilt with his claws and curled up. He blew a smoky breath over Kat's fingers. She gave a little smile and looked over at me. I smiled back, but that quickly slid off my face and landed with a splat on the floor when she spoke again.

'I think your grandad's right,' she said quietly.

I looked at her. Was she about to say what I thought she was about to say?

'I think it's time to let the dragons go.'

Yup.

I gaped at her. I waited for Ted and Kai to jump in and start protesting, like they had when I'd told them about the deal I'd made with Grandad. But this time neither of them said anything.

'Hang on a minute,' I said. 'A few days ago you were furious with me for even mentioning it.'

Kat sighed. 'I know,' she said. 'But things got pretty hairy at Halloween, and the truth is they've both been getting more . . .'

'Challenging.' Kai finished the sentence for her.

Kat nodded. 'The thing is, Tomas, however much we want to, I just don't think we *can* keep them any more,' she said sadly. 'Mum and Dad nearly found out about Crystal and Dodger.'

'It's easier for you – Flicker's still small,' said Kai.

'And he hasn't got someone winding him up all the time,' added Kat.

'Dodger used to do everything he could to hide from people, but it's like he's getting less afraid. Which is great in a way, but he's not being very careful. He keeps forgetting to blend.'

'The other day Dad came down to breakfast and found him sitting on his plate scoffing his toast. Dodger disappeared quick smart, and Mum didn't believe Dad of course, but then the next day she found claw marks in the butter. They've been acting really weird ever since.'

'And now Mum's decided it was rats and is going to get the pest control people in,' Kai said.

'What if they start putting poison down or something horrible?' said Kat.

I saw her shiver just at the thought.

'So maybe they should stay with me and Ted until things quieten down?' I suggested.

I turned to Ted, hoping he might back me up.

He looked shifty and started poking his tongue round his teeth – a thing he does when he's about to say something he knows you won't like.

'Actually, Sunny's been a bit of a handful too lately. I didn't want to say anything – because you all seemed to be getting on fine. But remember you told us how to deal with the poo? You know, get it down the loo quick so it doesn't dry out and explode. Well, Sunny poos a *lot*. And it must have caused a blockage. All the toilets started overflowing. Mum went in first with a plunger. But she couldn't clear it and had to call a plumber. And they found this . . . this . . . poo-berg.'

'What on earth is a poo-berg?' Kat said, her face screwed up in disgust.

'You know, like an iceberg but made of poo,' Ted said matter-of-factly. 'All this time we've been thinking the poo gets flushed away, but it's actually been collecting in the drains.'

'Are you saying there's a giant dragon poo somewhere under our feet, right now?' Kat said.

Ted nodded. 'Not just giant, it's enormous. Gigantinormous! And it's getting bigger all the time.'

We all stared down at the floor.

I pictured the carpet rupturing and a massive volcanic eruption with dragon poo raining down on the whole of our village. This was not good. Not good at all.

Kat sighed and Crystal flew down to land next to her. She stared into the little dragon's eyes. Crystal swept her head from side to side, sending out a gentle breath that frosted Kat's fringe. The delicate ice patterns made her hair all sparkly. Kat touched her head, looking sad.

'What if us keeping the dragons has somehow messed up their chances of flying off to where they ought to be?' she said quietly.

We all looked at each other and then at the dragons around us. I got the feeling this was something that had been playing on Kat's mind long before today. Could she be right? Had stopping these dragons leaving with the others made it so they wouldn't now be able to go home?

'We don't even know where the dragons go, do we?' Kat said. 'So it's not like we can take them there. And –' she paused, her voice hardly more than a whisper now – 'even if they do go – what if it's like when well-meaning people care for baby animals and then the parents or herd reject them?'

She was looking at me for reassurance, but I couldn't give her any. I was beginning to realise there was an awful lot we didn't know about dragons. So how could we hope to look after them properly?

I'd thought I knew everything about Flicker. But I hadn't even known that he could control the weather. Perhaps Kat was right, perhaps it *was* time to let the dragons go.

I looked down at Flicker curled in my lap now, his scales flickering turquoise and his little body sending a pulse of warmth right through me.

How could I ever say goodbye to him?

11
If Only Dragons Could Talk

One thing was clear, I had to find out more about the dragons. I had to know that if we were going to let them go, they would be OK.

'Sometimes I really wish dragons could talk,' I whispered to Flicker as we lay curled in bed. His eyes twinkled up at me and he let out a low rumble that I felt as a flutter inside my chest.

That night I had an incredibly vivid dream. I'd had this

same dream a few times now, and I didn't like it. It was different from my usual dream of volcanoes and glaciers. In this one I was flying over a forest. And dotted among the trees were clearings with buildings, like a hidden city. And suddenly I realised I was surrounded by dragons, all flying alongside me. Together we dived down towards the city and our flames scorched the land.

I woke up sweating, just when I had been about to swoop over the heads of this one little family, who were looking up at us, their hands raised.

I lay there, heart pounding. Every time I had this dream I couldn't help thinking about all the people in the city and wondering if the dragons had destroyed everything.

But tonight something else stuck in my mind. The image of the river winding its way through the forest. Suddenly I realised I knew that snaking outline. It was the river from the map I had found.

I switched on my lamp and looked at Flicker, who was shimmering through brilliant shades of red. It wasn't the first time he had shown me things in my dreams. Maybe he was trying to tell me something again? But what?

I jumped out of bed and scrabbled underneath, pulling out the map. Now, in case you haven't been following the whole story – which, believe me, you really should, otherwise you'll know even less about dragons than we do – this map had fallen out of *A World of Plants*, an encyclopedia that had belonged to Elvi Jónsdóttir, the old woman who'd lived in the house before Nana and Grandad.

Elvi had left quite a lot of stuff behind, most of it piled up in Grandad's shed. I'd already found boxes of things she'd brought back from her travels around the world. In one of these I'd discovered the tin of ash and her instructions about how much to sprinkle on the dragon-fruit tree to keep it healthy.

It was then I'd realised that she'd been looking after the tree, just like us. What I didn't know was whether she had ever seen the dragons. I'd always hoped she'd have more to tell me about where the dragon-fruit tree came from. But although the map was beautiful, all drawn within the outline of this dragon's wings, it hadn't given me any actual information.

But perhaps I was missing something.

I held it close and peered at it again.

My finger traced the river winding through the rainforest, pausing at the little clearings among the trees. There was no sign of any city here. Not like in my dream. I turned the map over. Nothing. Except some really faint marks, which were probably just stains from where something else had pressed against it. It was a miracle the map had survived as well as it had really – it was obviously ancient.

Flicker fluttered over and jiggled from foot to foot, prodding at the piece of paper in my hand. It

was like he could see something I couldn't.

Then all of a sudden he sneezed. I snatched the map out of the way just as a short fiery burst shot past it.

And then I blinked and shook my head. Just for a second I had seen something. Right there on the map.

'Hey, do that again, Flicker,' I whispered.

A ripple shimmered across his body. He stretched his wings and blew a gentle flickering flame. I held the map up in front of it. And I saw it again. The city from my dreams!

It was like turning on a light and suddenly seeing where you are. There were buildings, monuments, houses, a grand square, all there, glowing now within the forest. And with the help of Flicker's flame I could see more too. Tiny swirly words snaked their way along the dragon's wings that framed the map. I squinted, trying to make out what they said.

'*La Ciudad Oculta de los Dragones.*'

It was hopeless; everything was written in a language I couldn't read. As I scanned down, one word kept jumping out at me, a word that I did recognise.

Dragones.

12
Buried Treasure

The next day I raced across the park to Nana and Grandad's house. I needed to do some digging – digging that didn't involve weeds for once.

Usually Nana would spot me a mile away and be waving non-stop till I collapsed in the doorway, panting and clutching my side. But today the house was empty.

With Grandad still in hospital, Nana was spending her days at his bedside. Even though I'd known she might not be at home, it felt strange letting myself in through the side gate and being there without them. It was like someone had taken the batteries out of your favourite toy – it looked the same but it was no fun playing with it.

I kept my eyes turned away from the house and focused on the garden, pretending Nana and Grandad had just popped upstairs to check on Lolli or were sitting together listening to the radio in their comfy chairs.

The door of the shed creaked when I pushed it open and I got the familiar blast of dust and earthy compost that always made me sneeze. I gave Flicker a nervous look; I didn't want him having a sneezing fit. But he ignored me and flew past, landing on the handle of Grandad's spade. I didn't stop him. I was glad of the company.

A World of Plants lay where we'd left it. I flicked through the pages of the old book, hoping something else might be hidden inside, but there was nothing. Grandad had stacked boxes of Elvi's stuff under the counter and I started pulling them out. Seeing how much was crammed into them, looking through them was going to be a long job. Then, as I dragged the last box out, something weird caught my eye.

On the floor was a metal ring, not plain metal but carved. I reached across to get it and found it fastened to the wooden planks. As I pulled harder the floorboard beneath it began to lift. I sucked in a breath along with a lungful of dust and spluttered. Was this an actual secret hiding place?

I'd always dreamed of finding secret hiding places and buried treasure. Or tunnels that led to whole other worlds. Maybe I was going to crawl down and find myself somewhere where beetles were in charge, like in that book I'd read. It felt like the world had finally caught up with my imagination. My heart was leaping up as if it wanted to jump out of my mouth and take a look around.

Flicker fluttered past my head and landed by my hand, his nose wiggling into the gap. Whatever was down there, he seemed as keen to find out as I was.

I nearly didn't find out at all, because a spider the size of an octopus with the muscles of a wrestler marched out towards my hand. It stood there like a warrior guard sent to protect the hidden treasures. I'm not kidding – this spider had attitude. Thankfully it took one look at Flicker and obviously thought better of a fight. It waved a leg in the air and scuttled off.

But let's face it – you don't care about warrior spiders, do you? You want to know what was under Grandad's shed.

So here's the other thing about having an imagination like mine. As well as taking you to places you might not want to go – like fearing the worst when I heard about Grandad's accident – it can also lead to a fair bit of disappointment. For a start, it wasn't a tunnel at all. There was no way I could have crawled through the little gap once the floorboard had been lifted. And it certainly didn't lead anywhere. It was just a hole.

But not an empty hole. There was a tin box about as big as a large shoebox. The fact that someone had gone to such lengths to hide it stopped my disappointment about the lack of a beetle underworld in its tracks.

Carefully I lifted the box up and shuffled back out from under the counter. I sat with it perched on my lap, running my thumbnail around the lid, trying to unjam it. Finally there was a little squeak as it loosened. I raised the lid and peered inside. The treasure turned out to be a leather notebook and stacks and stacks of papers and photos in neat bundles, some black and white, old and faded, and others in colour, obviously more recent. And as it happened, this was way more valuable than any gold or diamonds.

I knew that as soon as I started looking through the first bundle of photos. Because every picture was of a different dragon. And what's more, they were all taken here in Grandad's garden.

A tiny yellow dragon perched on a bamboo cane. A long purple dragon with silver-tipped wings scratching at a pile of newspaper. Two dragons, one

scarlet and one gold with twisted
horns, curled up together on the
leaves of a bush. I stared at them one
after another, taking in every little
detail. Until I paused at one picture
of a midnight-blue dragon sitting

on an open hand. The hand was wrinkled, with gold
rings on three of the fingers, and there were fine blue

markings in a pattern around
the wrist, like a tattoo. And
when I looked at it closer I
saw that what I was looking
at was a dragon's tail.

Flicker's scales shone
gold like he had lit up inside, and if I'd had scales I'd

have been shining just as
brilliantly. I grinned. It suddenly
seemed pretty clear that Elvi
had absolutely known about
the dragons!

13
Daleks Don't Make Tea

Before I could look through another bundle, a shadow passed across the little window of the shed. I heard footsteps and something being dragged across the ground. With my heart still in my mouth from finding the box and its contents, at this point it basically jumped right out and legged it out of the shed, leaving me a total quivering wreck. I peered through the window and I bet you already know who I saw. Yup! Grim. Grandad was stuck in hospital and here was Grim snooping round his garden, getting up to who knows what.

I jumped up and stomped outside, banging open the shed door as I went. To say Grim looked a bit startled is like saying a T-rex is a bit fierce. He nearly leaped off the ground.

When he came back down to earth, he let out a huff and then nodded at me. Then he carried on pushing Grandad's wheelbarrow.

'Those bean plants need to come out,' he said over his shoulder.

Hello? I'd just caught him trespassing and all he could offer was beans?

I gave him my best threatening glare, complete with laser stabbing eyes, but since he wasn't looking my way any more it didn't do a lot of good. I hurried after him.

'My grandad's not here,' I managed to say.

'Nope,' he answered.

'He's in hospital,' I added, hoping to make him feel guilty for stamping round his garden.

'He is,' he said. He let the wheelbarrow drop and turned to face me.

'I thought it best I give a hand while he's not about,' he said. 'So he don't worry about things going to ruin.'

Hang on a minute – was Grim saying he was here to help? He'd spent enough time scowling over the fence at us that I couldn't quite believe he had it in him.

'I can look after things,' I said fiercely. 'Grandad knows I will. And he'll be back soon anyway. Mum said he's doing really well,' I added.

'Oh aye,' said Grim. 'I'm sure you're right. Though now there's his heart to think about, I don't think he'll be lugging this here wheelbarrow round for a bit.'

His heart? No one had said anything to me about that.

He'd had a funny turn with his heart a few years ago – I'd always worried that running round after me had brought it on. I'd been poorly when I was little and Nana and Grandad had looked after me quite a lot. But Grandad had always insisted it was more likely that my funny heart had just made his heart laugh so much it had turned it funny too, and not to worry about it.

'What do you mean?' I blurted. 'There's nothing wrong with his heart. It's just his hip they've got to fix. That's all.'

For a second Grim looked uncomfortable. He coughed, which anyone knows is just a really rubbish way of buying some time while you think of what to say.

I could feel myself getting crosser by the second. Here he was acting like he knew more than me about Grandad.

Grim bent down and pulled a few weeds out and chucked them in the barrow.

'Like you say, he'll be back. Just thought I'd lend a hand in the meantime.'

Grim being helpful and nice went against everything I'd ever thought about him. My brain whirred, trying to process this new information, and then simply clunked to a stop. Nope – Grim being nice didn't compute.

But then a thought sneaked in somewhere at the back of my mind – it sat there muttering away like the most annoying kid in class. And if I strained really hard I thought I could hear it saying, 'Excuse me, but haven't you been wrong about Grim in the past?'

You see, we'd thought he'd been cheating his way to victory in the flower-and-vegetable competition. I'd been all set to accuse him of using chemicals and killing the dragon-fruit tree when in fact it had been Liam's dragon super-sizing his onions. All Grim had done was play music to his vegetables, thinking that was the secret of his success.

Still, I couldn't get my head round this new neighbourly Grim. It was like a Dalek suddenly offering you a cup of tea. And if you've got any sense, if you come across one of those, the best thing to do is make a hasty escape – which is exactly what I did.

14
La Ciudad Oculta de los Dragones

Later on I sat with the others, squashed in the den with the dragons perched on branches around us. The box of photos lay on the ground.

They were staring at me and I could hear the clanking of their brain cogs working through everything I'd just told them.

'So she did know about the dragons?' Kat said smiling. 'I'm glad. It means she wasn't on her own after all.'

I nodded. We'd all felt a bit sad for Elvi after hearing that when she'd died there had been no one

to sort through her belongings. 'No, I reckon she had plenty of company. There are ten dragons in these pictures at least.'

Ted held up another photo, ready to read out snippets of what Elvi had written on the back. She'd studied the dragons in meticulous detail, recording how big they were, what they ate, how they interacted with each other, where they chose to hide out, how fast they were, how long they stayed. It went on and on. The old woman was getting a big thumbs up from Ted, with his love of facts.

Next to him, Kai held the map up, turning it over in his hands. 'And this city just appeared when Flicker blew on it?' he asked, still not able to believe it.

'Well, not *on* it. If he'd done that it'd be a pile of ash. I was holding it up just in front of the flame.'

'And you saw it?' Kai went on. 'You saw the city?'

I nodded, unable to keep the grin off my face. 'It was right there. *La Ciudad Oculta de los Dragones* – the Hidden Dragon City.'

I'd looked it up. There was nothing more about the place itself, but it'd been easy enough to get a translation by typing the words into my computer.

'So you think she went looking for this Hidden City?' he asked.

'I don't know,' I said. 'That's why I want to take a closer look at these.'

I pointed to the photos, the bundles of papers and the notebook that Kat was now leafing through. 'I'm hoping all this might tell us something.'

'This looks like a diary,' Kat said, squinting at the tiny scrawl, 'but her writing's even smaller than mine. That's one way to keep it private, I guess.'

'Let me have a look,' Kai said. 'Her handwriting can't be worse than yours and I'm used to deciphering that.'

Kat looked about to object but then shrugged and handed it over.

I reached down and picked up one of the bundles of photos. These all seemed to be of the same trip – to a dense rainforest.

I held a wad of them and flicked through. It reminded me of one of those cartoons you can make, where the pictures blur into a moving image. Seeing them rush past almost felt like I was watching a movie of Elvi's journey.

Here was the boat she'd arrived on, the matted forest she'd trekked through and local people she'd met along the way. But there were also lorries piled high with sawn logs and stretches of road cutting a straight path through the trees.

As the photos went on there were more and more close-ups of tiny creatures, beautiful flowers and also one particular man. He had dark wavy hair and a neatly cropped beard and moustache, and in every picture he was smiling. I could almost see the same twinkle I saw in Grandad's eyes shining out from the photographs. I imagined being in his shoes, exploring deeper into the forest, not knowing what I might find there. And how exciting that must have felt.

Had Elvi and this man really been searching for the Hidden City – and had they found it?

Eagerly I started going through more bundles of photos. More forest, more birds, more photos of the man and finally a few of Elvi herself. Either everyone she met was especially tall or Elvi was tiny. Her white-blonde hair was pulled back loosely, and there was something about the look she gave the photographer that made you suspect she'd just dropped a centipede down their back and was dying to burst out laughing and tell them.

Then I came to one of her standing in front of an enormous tree trunk. She was smiling and her arm was stretched out as if she was pointing to something down behind her. I peered closer and could see that in among the tangle of tree roots and vegetation there was what looked like a small pile of rubble. It might not seem like much to get excited about. But if you'd been looking for evidence of a lost civilisation, I reckon the sight of rubble in such dense forest would probably warrant a

bit of a grin. And when I saw the next picture I'd have
bet her grin got even wider.

I leaped up, waving the photo and startling Sunny
into unleashing a fiery belch that almost set it alight.

'I've got something!' I cried.

It was a picture of Elvi standing in front of a wall,
and the expression on her face seemed to scream, 'I
told you so!' The huge stone blocks of the wall fitted
together like one of those wooden puzzles you get at
Christmas. And carved into the stone was an enormous
dragon's head.

15
Missing Pieces

'Whoa,' whispered Ted.

I turned the picture over and squinted at the date written on the back.

'Hey, Kai, look up 28 April.'

Kai riffled through the notebook. 'Got it,' he said.

And we all crowded round to hear what she had written on that day.

'*We are here. Finally, after all this time, Arturo and I have found it– . . . La Ciudad Oculta de los Dragones. We have been searching for so long. And we were right to believe.*'

'It must have felt amazing,' said Kat.

'Shhh,' snapped Kai. 'There's more. She says: *We are walking through the ruins of a city where people and dragons lived cheek by jowl.*'

'What's a jowl?' asked Ted.

I had no idea, but my dream flashed into my mind, the family with their hands raised. Maybe it was some kind of weapon?

'I think it means dragons and people lived side by side,' said Kat.

'Are you done?' asked Kai. He scowled at us and cleared his throat, ready to continue.

'*According to the stories Arturo grew up with, it was in this place that dragons breathed upon the forest, burning the land and reigniting the life within it. And in return the citizens of the city guarded the dragon-fruit trees and celebrated and protected the dragons.*'

My stomach lurched, as if I had wings again and was soaring over the heads of the family. I looked down at them, at their raised hands. And then it hit me. Of course! Those people weren't cowering in fear. They were waving. Welcoming the dragons!

Grandad had told me once how forest fires bring new growth and how sometimes farmers even set fire to their land on purpose to reinvigorate it. The dragons must have been doing that for the people of this place.

We all looked at each other and grinned. As if picking up on our excitement, Crystal, Dodger, Sunny and Flicker sent a spray of sparks glittering into the air around us.

'Keep going. What else does she say?' Kat urged.

'Arturo fears that we will not be the last to find the city, now the roads are cutting through the forest. I expect he is right. This Hidden City may not stay hidden for much longer.'

'But it did stay hidden, didn't it?' said Ted. 'I mean, you said there was nothing about it when you looked it up.'

I shook my head. 'No, it looks like they managed to keep it secret after all.'

'I wonder what happened to the city?' Kat said. 'Why it fell into such ruin. Do you think the dragons left?'

I shrugged. 'I don't know. Maybe. Maybe something else happened. I don't suppose we'll ever know. It must have been such a long time ago.'

Kai flicked further through the notebook, squinting at Elvi's tiny handwriting. We all waited. I actually wanted to grab it out of his hand he was taking so long. But since I had struggled to read it in the first place I jammed my hands under my bum to stop myself.

'Here you go. This is from a couple of months later.'

'I do not want to leave. Especially now when we have found there is more to this place than stories. And I do not want to leave Arturo. But this is not my home. And England is not Arturo's. So we have said our goodbyes. But because of him I am taking this most precious of things with me.'

'What did she take?' Kat said.

Kai unstuck a piece of paper from the notebook. 'I don't know. But look, there's a letter.'

My dearest Elvi,
We did it! You and I. Thank you for believing. I must stay and protect the Hidden City and keep its secrets now more than ever. But thanks to what we have found, there will be hope in two places. One day there will be dragons again – I truly believe it. The world needs dragons
Your friend,
Arturo

'What does that mean?'

'More than stories? Found what? What did they find? Do you think they found dragons there?' Kat asked, her excitement bubbling over into a torrent of questions.

'I don't think so,' I said. 'I bet they're talking about the dragon-fruit tree.'

'I can't see her bringing that back in her suitcase,' Ted said.

'Well, no, but she could have brought back a cutting or even a fruit and grown the tree here.'

The others nodded.

'But what made them think that was even possible? They must have found some evidence that dragons really had existed – and that they could again.'

We all looked at each other. There was so much we didn't know. It was like being given the coolest jigsaw ever and finding that so many pieces were missing, you ended up with just sky and one tantalising glimpse of some mysterious shape.

But, with Ted's stomach rumbling and the dragons getting fidgety, searching for the missing pieces was just going to have to wait.

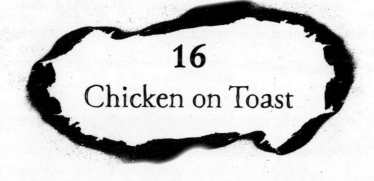

16
Chicken on Toast

You know how my mum often brings home pets to look after? Those ferrets for a start. Well, they've gone, thank goodness. But we've still got the cockatoo, so it didn't surprise me that much to find a chicken sitting on the toaster when I got in. I was a bit more

surprised by the gaggle of gulls squabbling in the downstairs loo. But it wasn't totally unheard of. So I grabbed a handful of biscuits and headed upstairs.

I thought I heard a gobbling noise coming from the airing cupboard on the landing, but with Flicker wriggling in my pocket I didn't have time to stop and check that one out.

Safe in my room, Flicker fluttered around stretching his wings and then settled down in the shoebox under my bed.

I lay back and imagined walking with Elvi and Arturo through the dense rainforest. What other secrets had they discovered hidden in that place? I'd left the notebook with Kai, who was the best at deciphering Elvi's writing. If anyone could tell us more about the dragons, I now knew it was Elvi.

Later I met Dad coming out of the lounge, and for once he wasn't wearing headphones. Which was actually weirder than seeing the turkey that suddenly strutted past us wearing a pair of Lolli's pants on its head.

'Can you hear that?' Dad asked.

'You mean the turkey?' I said, watching it disappear into the kitchen.

Dad looked at me like I was barmy. He'd obviously missed the turkey completely.

'No, that sound.'

I screwed up my ears, which is harder than screwing up your eyes and involves more of your face. Nope. I couldn't hear anything.

'Maybe it's the heating,' I offered. 'I hear it whistling sometimes, when I'm in bed.'

'It's not a whistle. It's more like a . . . a song.'

My eyes shot up to the ceiling and Lolli's room above. Was Tinkle singing? I couldn't hear anything, but then Dad had ears like one of those bat-eared foxes. Having a job in music had definitely sensitised him. He could hear an ant fart in next door's garden through double glazing.

I shrugged. Dad waggled his finger in his ear like he thought there was something in there that he could fish out.

He shook his head and wandered off down the hall, muttering about insuring his ears and seeing the doctor to check for signs of tinnitus, whatever that was.

I headed upstairs and stuck my head round Lolli's door. She'd made a nest of cushions on the floor, and her duvet and a sheet had been pulled over the back of a chair. Mum was used to building her hideouts – under Lolli's strict supervision of course. I crawled in and found Lolli tucked up with Tinkle on her lap. She was chatting to the little dragon as if Tinkle could understand every word.

Flicker had followed me in and now hopped over onto Lolli's lap. He and Tinkle greeted each other by bending their heads forward and crossing necks so each of them rested their head on the other's shoulder. Flicker's scales shone brilliantly as he started changing colour. It always felt like looking at him through a kaleidoscope when he did this, the glittering colours falling away in a never-ending shimmer. Only this time he finally settled on a bright moonlight silver with flecks of blue, as if he was trying to match Tinkle. As they curled up together, Flicker wrapped his tail around Tinkle, keeping her close.

Something wriggled under one of the cushions. A claw peeked out and for a second I thought Lolli had gone and hatched another dragon. But then I saw a little yellow feathery head. It was a baby chick. And when I lifted the cushion further I saw three more fluffy faces, their beaks open wide.

'I think we'd better take these downstairs,' I said, remembering the chicken on the toaster. 'Their mum's probably looking for them.'

Lolli nodded.

'Moo,' she said, and pointed out the window.

'No cows out there, Lollibob.'

Lolli shook her head and frowned. Sometimes I had the feeling she thought I was just plain dim.

'A moo,' she said again. And then waggled her arms like a chicken.

Usually I was pretty good at working out what Lolli was saying, but this had me stumped. I wasn't quite sure what a cow had to do with a nest of chicks or why it might need wings.

I understood a bit more at teatime. We'd just finished Mum's not entirely successful attempt at shepherd's pie – frankly the shepherd could have it back. We were about to face a cheesecake that I could clearly see had nothing to do with cheese or cake and I knew for a fact shouldn't be dribbling off the plate.

Mum poured a slice onto Dad's plate and then shrieked, just as Lolli cried, 'Moo!' Dad, who was already nervous from looking at the dessert he was going to have to eat, jumped a mile.

I stared as they all pointed out the patio doors. Running across the garden was a huge long-necked bird with flames bursting from its tail feathers.

'Oh,' I said, finally understanding. 'Emu.'

Lolli nodded, satisfied that at last someone had listened.

The emu, chickens, turkey and gulls weren't the only feathery friends we'd suddenly acquired. Along with the resident cockatoo, there were at least sixty pigeons on the roof, dozens of ducks and geese on the lawn and the trees were chock-full of starlings, blackbirds, sparrows and goodness knows what else.

'There's that song again,' Dad cried. 'Come on, you lot, you've got to be able to hear that?'

This time, above the cheeping, squawking, clucking and quacking, I could definitely make out the sound of Tinkle singing.

Lolli's dragon might not be causing mayhem with sparks and flames, but compared to the mess her new feathered friends were making, cleaning up after Flicker was a piece of cake.

17
The Seed of an Idea

After finding the photos and Elvi's diary we stopped talking about letting the dragons go. We'd all decided we couldn't do that. Not yet. At least not until we knew more.

As soon as I saw Kat and Kai in the cloakroom outside our class I knew they had found something important. They were pretty much glowing with excitement. While everyone else piled in to take their seats, they pulled Ted and me to one side.

'You were right, Tomas,' hissed Kat. 'Elvi *was* talking about the tree. That is what she brought back.'

'Well, the seed of the tree,' corrected Kai. 'In the city, she and Arturo found this temple, and inside that they discovered the map you have and –'

'And . . . and . . . a golden dragon's foot with a seed on two of its claws,' spluttered Kat.

Kai glared at his twin. 'We agreed *I* was going to tell them. I found it out.'

'Oh all right, go on then,' she said sulkily.

Ted's eyes were growing wider by the second as we waited for Kai to continue.

'There was writing carved into the stone around the dragon's foot. It said they were the last active dragon-fruit seeds. That the trees that grew from them would grow dragons. Arturo kept one and gave one to Elvi. That's what he meant about there being hope in two places.'

'But his didn't grow,' said Kat.

'Why? What happened to it?' Ted demanded.

Kai shrugged. 'They have all these theories, but they don't know for sure.'

'And then something terrible happened,' Kat said in little more than a squeak. 'Elvi's letters to Arturo started going unanswered.'

I stared at Kat, whose eyes were shining.

'She flew back to Mexico to find him, but all anyone could tell her was that he had walked into the forest one day and never returned,' she said.

I pictured Arturo's wavy dark hair against the green of the forest, and his twinkling eyes. I think we were all thinking the same thing. That we had only just met Arturo, but his story was now part of ours too. And we weren't ready to say goodbye. We had barely said hello properly.

'I'd like to have met him – and Elvi,' Kat said quietly.

'They were pretty awesome,' Ted agreed. 'Proper explorers.'

Kai and I nodded. And then Kai said, 'And you haven't heard the half of it.'

'Wait till you hear this,' Kat said.

Elvi waited ten years before the tree was big enough to grow fruit,' he said. 'Ten years! And then at last the dragons came. Can you imagine waiting that long for anything?'

I couldn't – but then I had trouble waiting till lunchtime to get the chocolate crackle surprise on that day's menu.

'So from then on Elvi was hatching dragons?' I asked.

Kai nodded. 'After that first crop she planted some of the seeds from the fruits that had grown. But only one of those seeds grew into a tree – it sounds like dragon-fruit trees are pretty hard to grow. Then she waited *another* ten years, looking after that new tree. But the second tree never grew dragons. And even when she took cuttings, the new trees that grew didn't have dragons either. The fruit just stayed normal fruit.'

'How come?'

'She never knew that either. But it means the tree in your grandad's garden is more important than ever. It's the last active dragon-fruit tree *anywhere*. She keeps saying how if there is only this one tree, there may not be a future for the dragons. Without Arturo there was no one else to help her. And she didn't ever tell anyone else, as she was afraid other people would take the dragons and the tree away. She felt it was up to her to protect the tree and look after the dragons.'

'And now it's up to us,' I said weakly. 'No pressure then.'

Kat started jiggling up and down manically.

'But I figured something out,' she said. 'I think I know why the second tree never grew dragons.'

'Why?' I asked, my head still spinning from everything they'd just said.

'The legend, remember? In Elvi's encyclopedia. It said the dragons breathe out the dragon fruits.'

'Yeah. So?' said Ted.

'Maybe the legend got it wrong. Miss Logan was telling us how stories change over time. Bits get added or forgotten. It could have got altered sometime in the retelling. What if it's not that they breathed the fruit *out*? What if they breathed *on* it and that's what turns a normal fruit into an active fruit – one that has seeds that grow into a tree that hatches dragons?'

'But that doesn't make sense. There were plenty of dragons in the garden – why didn't *they* activate the seeds?' Ted asked.

Kat's shoulders suddenly sagged. She looked at Kai, but he just shrugged.

'I hadn't thought of that,' she said flatly.

'Maybe it takes a particular dragon,' I said quietly. 'I mean all our dragons seem to have their own special ability. Maybe there was a dragon that activated the tree?'

Before I could say anything else, there was the sound of a toilet flushing and Mahid, a boy in our class, appeared from round the corner. We all kept silent and pretended to look for Kai's supposedly missing gloves.

As Mahid disappeared into class, Kat whispered, 'You don't think he overheard anything, do you?'

'I doubt it, but if he did, we'll just pretend we were talking about a book we've been reading.'

It was only when we'd taken our seats that I saw someone else come in from around the corner. Someone who'd been in the toilets this whole time and who could have heard every word we'd said. Someone who would know it was no story book we were talking about.

And that someone was the King of Trouble.

18
A Slippery Customer

All day I watched the clock above Miss Logan's desk. I couldn't wait to get home and check on Flicker. Lately he'd been spending more time perched on the windowsill, staring up at the sky. I was feeling less and less like leaving him on his own while I was out. But when Mum met me after school, I found myself being dragged to the shops. She was on a mission. And all because of the Juicer.

She'd decided that as winter loomed everyone in the family needed more than just five-a-day of fruit and veg. Apparently we needed a full vitamin and mineral body armour to combat the army of bugs that always struck at this time of year. And this meant that as well as Grandad's ample fruit-and-veg boxes – stuffed with spinach, broccoli, apples and pears – she intended to stock up on anything he wasn't growing. And with the Juicer we were going to get all the green super-shakes we could want. Which in my case was none.

Standing at the back of Herb's Fruit and Veg Shop, I listened to her read out her long list of must-haves. This was going to take a while. I'd just started building a Brussels-sprout mountain when I saw Liam come into the shop. I wriggled down behind some crates of bananas.

Herb's assistant Mandy greeted Liam and then bent to listen as he started whispering something. She straightened up and shook her head, looking confused. He started waving his hands about like he was drawing something in the air. She shook her head again and shrugged. Whatever he'd asked her about, the answer was obviously no.

He scowled and stomped out of the shop, muttering under his breath.

I resisted the urge to run straight over and quiz Mandy. I'd watched enough spy shows to know that if you want someone to give up some vital piece of information, you have to act all nonchalant, like you don't really care.

I sauntered over. And slipped on one of the bananas. It was hard to act nonchalant when you'd just landed flat on your face.

'Er . . . hello,' I said, wiping smooshed banana off my forehead and rubbing at the rapidly appearing lump.

'Can I help you?' she asked.

'I just . . . you know . . . saw my old mate Liam. He looked a bit . . . you know . . . put out, you know . . . fed up . . . you know?'

She looked out the door and then back at me, one eyebrow wiggling up towards her curly mop of red hair.

'Oh, him,' she said. 'Bit of a grump, your mate, isn't he?'

I smiled and nodded sympathetically.

'Got all stroppy just because we didn't have any of these weird fruit he was looking for. I told him I haven't even heard of them, let alone seen one.'

'Weird fruit?' I asked.

But – let's face it – I already knew what was coming.

'Yeah, he wanted some dragon-fruit thing. The way he described it, I told him someone must be pulling his leg. I've never seen anything looking like that.'

And she headed off towards a lady who was loudly sniffing lemons. While I stood there looking a bit of a lemon myself, with my mouth hanging open. All I could picture was Liam with arms full of dragon fruits.

'You don't think he's trying to grow himself another super-sized dragon, do you?' asked Kai when I met up with the others later.

'Well, he won't have much luck, will he? Not with a fruit he's picked up in a shop. He must know there won't be a dragon growing in one of those,' answered Kat.

'Even he can't be that clueless,' I said. 'No, he'd need to get at our tree for that, and there's no way he can get anywhere close again. Not after I convinced Grandad to put up some wire along the hedge to stop him sneaking back in.'

'Maybe he thinks if he plants some seeds his dragon will make them grow super-fast and that then he'll have his very own dragon tree,' suggested Kai.

'That's all we need,' said Ted.

Kat snorted. 'Well, it won't matter if he does. He won't grow dragons, will he? We know that. I mean Elvi didn't have any luck. Ours is the only active dragon-fruit tree there is.'

I nodded.

'I think we need to start keeping an even closer eye on him though. Till we know for sure what he's up to.'

'That's easier said than done when you've already got both eyes keeping watch on these two,' she said, pointing up to Crystal and Dodger who were locked in a friendly but explosive battle of ice blast and fire.

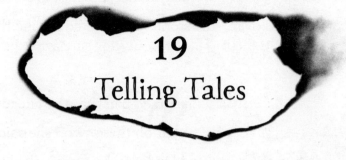

19
Telling Tales

Back at home I pulled out one of the bundles of papers I'd found alongside Elvi's diary. I undid the string and laid out the sheets across my bed. There had to be more she could tell us about the Hidden City and the dragons. But it made my eyes hurt trying to decipher it all.

Most of it was detailed travel arrangements, lists of equipment and sketches and descriptions of flowers and insects that they came across – many that had never been recorded before. Elvi was interested and excited about everything they saw. But every so often she would pause in this daily detail and these were the parts I pored over – the stories they shared around the fire in the evening.

Arturo has kept everyone enthralled as usual. Telling the tales his grandfather told him, of the dragons that were born in this forest. And how the people shared a special bond with them. Their fire helped the land stay rich and fertile. But the dragons never stayed for longer than a few months. The climate was too hot. Dragon flame and fiery equatorial heat were an explosive mix. As they got bigger the dragons grew restless and began to leave.

But occasionally dragons would bond with people and would stay longer. Then it was no longer safe for the people or the dragons. Fires burned out of control and the dragon who had stayed grew sick.

Today we found carvings on the stone walls of the city. Showing people watching the dragons soaring to the stars.

Arturo told me how whenever he heard this part of the story he had always wondered where the dragons flew to. Until he met me. For this is where our two histories collide. Ever since I told him about the stories my own mother and grandparents told me, of long-ago dragons flying over the grass-roofed homes of our village and settling in the volcanoes of the far north, we have known we hold two parts of the same story.

I collected up all the loose papers, put them back in the tin box with the photos and curled up in bed. I thought of the dragons that had stayed too long and got sick. Would that happen to Flicker? Elvi had said it was the heat of the rainforest that was the problem. And it made sense. The dragon-fruit tree needed heat to grow and thrive, but as they grew the dragons needed a colder place to live.

Looking out the window at the drizzle, it was hard

to believe our weather would cause Flicker a problem.
But what if it did?

I watched him on the windowsill, his tail flicking
back and forth as he blew a misty breath across the
glass. I reached out my hand and he flew back to me,
his spray of sparks twinkling across my room. When
he curled up next to me I allowed his warm breath to
blow my worries away.

Later though, when I met up with the others and I read them the passages, everyone went super-quiet. Since finding Elvi's diary our plans to let the dragons go had been lost in the excitement of learning more about them.

But Kat took this new information as further proof that it was the right thing to do.

'It's just too risky keeping them here,' she said.

'We need a proper plan then,' Kai replied.

'Yeah,' agreed Ted. 'It's not like we can just open the window and they'll fly off any more.'

'That's because Sunny knows you've got a room full of chocolate and crisps,' Kai laughed. 'He's hardly likely to give all that up in a hurry.'

Ted looked a bit sheepish but didn't disagree.

'Tomas, we need to get all of them to your grandad's garden when the next crop of dragons hatches,' said Kat. 'They'll be able to follow the others then.'

'Are there any new fruits?' Kai asked.

I nodded, the familiar squirmy feeling in my tummy returning at the thought that our time with the dragons might be over.

'There's been another crop of fruits ripening over the past week,' I said.

'Good,' said Kat. 'With any luck it'll only be a few days before we have some new dragons in the garden.'

'And it's Bonfire Night on Saturday,' Kai added. 'It's perfect timing. With all the fireworks going off no one's going to notice our lot, even with their crackling sparks and fiery belches.'

He was right, it was the perfect opportunity. But that didn't make the thought of it any easier.

20
Time to Let Go

However many times you see a dragon hatch out of a dragon fruit, it never gets old. I mean, how could it? The red fruit, the hint of a glow, watching and waiting for the spiky leaves to start bulging. Knowing it could happen at any moment, but always jumping in surprise when the POP finally happens and the tiny dragon shoots out. Then peering down at them as they stretch their wings and shake their heads and let out their first spark or puff of smoke or frosty breath. Each one different, from long and slender to tiny and plump, from pale grey to the brightest orange and with wings every colour of the rainbow. All of them special. There's never going to be anything other than magic in the air when a dragon hatches.

But on Saturday as we met in Grandad's garden the excitement was overshadowed by the knowledge of what we were about to do.

As we stood around the dragon-fruit tree watching the newly hatched dragons, we all looked as miserable as each other.

I lifted my hand and a tiny midnight-blue dragon fluttered onto my fingers. It tilted its head from side to side and then hiccupped out a smoky breath.

'It's got twinkly horns like Tinkle,' Kat said sadly.

'Hang on,' said Kai. 'Where is Tinkle?'

Everyone had been too busy with their dragons to notice Tinkle was missing, but now Ted, Kat and Kai were all looking at me, their brows wrinkling.

'Lolli isn't feeling well,' I said quickly. 'I couldn't take Tinkle away from her when she was all tucked up in bed feeling miserable. There'll still be dragons hatching tomorrow. I'll bring Tinkle then.'

Kat frowned but there wasn't much she could do. I think she knew that if we didn't go ahead right

now, everyone might just change their minds.

'So who's going first?' Ted asked as he cradled a glowing Sunny in his arms.

'I think they should all go together,' said Kai.

A pair of green-winged dragons that had just hatched zipped back and forth above our heads.

'None of them seem very interested in leaving, if you ask me,' said Ted.

We already knew that sometimes the dragons hung around – we'd seen enough evidence of the mess they made to know that. But we didn't understand why sometimes they flew off straight away and other times they stayed longer. I'd always thought it was to stock up on some food – and by that I mean demolishing Grim's vegetable patch. But we'd seen enough dragons hatch and take off by now to know that this wasn't always the case.

Typically, on this night when we really needed them to head up into the sky and lead our dragons away, none of them were budging. There were now seven or eight little dragons zooming about from Grim's garden to Grandad's. Grim's winter lettuces were taking a particular battering and I winced at the thought of him finding the wreckage the next day.

'Let's try encouraging them,' said Kat. 'Let your dragons go on the count of three, and we'll herd them all upwards.'

It turned out to be more like on the count of thirty, because every time Kat got to 'three' someone held onto their dragon, unable to let it go at the last minute.

'Come on, you lot, we need to do this,' Kat said. 'I'm going to count one more time. No messing about.'

And knowing Kat meant business, this time we finally did it. We let our dragons go.

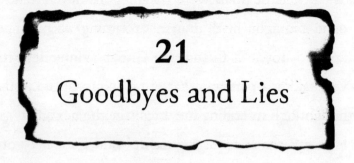

21
Goodbyes and Lies

It wasn't quite the farewell we'd imagined. In fact, Crystal, Sunny, Dodger and Flicker didn't go further than the apple tree. They perched there looking at us and at the newly hatched dragons zipping round the garden. A lame bit of hand-flapping did nothing to help.

I looked up into the cloudy sky, wondering what else we could do. Suddenly a firework exploded somewhere in the distance. A glittering sparkle of green and red. The next second, I heard the whistling of one of those ones that shoots way up high. It hung in the air like a burning star before the bang came.

It had obviously got the dragons' attention. An orange dragon with purple and green wings sped upwards towards the light. It let out a spray of sparks that just for an instant formed a halo around the bright firework. I watched the dragon soaring higher and higher. Perhaps it was leaving at last.

But then the glittering of the firework fizzled out and the dragon stopped in its tracks. It hovered in mid-air, its head flicking from side to side as if it was searching for the bright light. As the cloudy sky grew dim again the dragon headed down to the garden and settled back on the lettuces.

Another bright light exploded, this time in my head. I glanced across at Flicker, remembering him perched on my windowsill. I could still see the fiery glow he had traced around the North Star.

'I think I know why they're not leaving!' I called to the others. 'They need to follow the North Star. And it's too cloudy tonight to see it. That must be why sometimes they hang around.'

'What? So we have to wait for a clear night?' asked Ted.

'Not if Flicker can help,' I replied. I held out my arm and waited for the ruby shimmering shape of my little dragon to come to me. He perched there, his head tilted to one side while I ran my fingers along his spines.

'Any chance of a little breeze to blow those clouds away?' I said. And then I bent closer and whispered something else, aware that Kat was watching me. Flicker's scales rippled scarlet and he launched upwards. Straight away we felt the air around us change. Leaves

rustled, the hedgerow shook and the trees began to creak and groan. As Flicker twirled and spun above us, the wind whirled faster and faster. Soon we had to shout above the gale.

'It's working,' Kat cried. And we looked up to see a sliver of moon appear through the clouds. And then there was the North Star. A brilliant point of light, like a beacon.

As soon as the sky was clear, a few dragons started flying up higher than they had been. We raced around the garden herding the stragglers. And then we called our dragons.

Sunny, Crystal and Dodger circled our heads for a few moments. Then Crystal twirled and dived down towards Kat, decorating the air with delicate icy patterns. They hung in front of us like intricate snowflakes before falling to the ground. Then she blew out a frosty breath that left Kat covered in glittering sparkles. Kat lifted a shining hand and I heard her whisper, 'It's OK, it's time to go home.' Sending one last icy spray over Kat, the purple dragon turned to look upwards and rose up into the sky.

Sunny was glowing like a burning torch. He dived down and plucked the half-eaten chocolate from Ted's hands, then belched a fiery breath that set light to the leaves above Ted's head. Ted laughed and danced out of the way as Sunny soared skywards.

'Imagine the flames

that'll come out of him when he's fully grown,' he said. 'Probably best to see that from a distance though!'

'Where's Dodger?' cried Kai. 'Has he gone already?'

We scanned the sky. Kai's shoulders sagged.

'I thought he might be a *bit* sorry to go,' he said.

Kat put her arm around him and I saw that the tears shining on her face had frozen like tiny diamonds from Crystal's icy breath.

And then Kai shrieked and jumped away from her. A blast of flame shot through his legs, singeing his trousers. Dodger flared fluorescent green, dived down, nipped Kai on the nose and sped away. Kai laughed and chased after him, waving madly at the disappearing shape.

Now there was just Flicker, still spinning in the air above us.

Gradually, he slowed and I felt my friends moving closer. They knew how hard this moment was going to be for me. But instead of rising up into the sky, Flicker fluttered back down towards us.

Everyone looked at me.

'What's going on?' said Ted. 'Why isn't Flicker going too?'

I turned and saw Kat's eyes narrowing, beaming out their laser rays, waiting for me to answer.

My tongue was stuck to the roof of my mouth, which was drier than the hottest desert right now. I tried my best to form words, but the voice that came out sounded like a squeak.

'I don't know,' I croaked. 'Maybe it's Tinkle not being here.'

'You *knew* that was going to happen,' Kat said crossly. 'You knew he wouldn't go without her.'

I spluttered my denial, shaking my head madly.

Kat was getting crosser by the second, and Ted and Kai were glaring at me, their jaws clamped shut.

'Look, it's OK. I'll send them off tomorrow,' I said quickly. 'There'll still be dragons hatching. I'll bring them both then.'

No one looked very impressed, but in the end, much to my surprise, they didn't give me a hard time. I think they were all just too upset about saying goodbye to their own dragons.

On the walk home no one said anything. All you could hear was our feet slapping the pavement, sounding out a sorrowful march. I could feel something lodged in my throat and with every step and heartfelt

sigh from the others the lump grew bigger. And bigger. Until I swallowed it down and it sat in my chest where it carried on growing.

And that something wasn't a piece of my mum's leaden roly-poly pudding, it was a big nasty lump of guilt. Because as you might have already guessed, Lolli wasn't really poorly at all. She was bouncing around quite happily at home. I'd seen how Flicker looked after Tinkle – keeping a watchful diamond eye on her just like I watched out for Lolli, and I'd known he wouldn't go anywhere without her.

For the first time ever I had properly lied to the superhero squad. Because the truth was, I had never intended to let Flicker and Tinkle go.

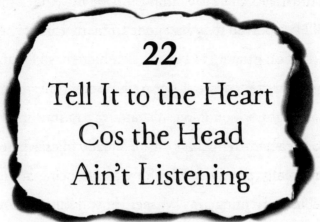

22
Tell It to the Heart Cos the Head Ain't Listening

Over the next few days I spent most of my time trying to avoid Ted, Kat and Kai. They'd believed me when I told them I had let Flicker and Tinkle go the following day, like I'd promised I would. But I didn't trust myself not to give the game away. With every day that passed they missed their dragons more – and even Kat was beginning to question whether it had all needed to happen quite so soon.

Every time I looked at Flicker now I felt an equal dose of relief and guilt. I couldn't imagine going to sleep at night without him curled up next to me, warming my dreams. But I knew that must be how the others had felt too. And they had gone through with it.

I was desperate to keep Flicker hidden, so I mainly only let him fly around my room. Sometimes I crept out at night, when it wasn't raining too much. After school, when the others headed over to the park, I raced home to be with him.

But something was wrong. He still fluttered over to greet me, but I could see that his bright red scales were becoming duller somehow. More and more often he was just staying a pale grey colour. And unless I fed him the broccoli stalks by hand, he didn't seem to be eating much either.

Every night since we had let the dragons go I had had the same dream. I was back in the land of fire and ice, but this time there was more. Sometimes a dream can feel so real it's hard to believe it isn't happening. I was flying again – seeing the world through a dragon's eyes – and it was so vivid I could almost feel the wind on my face.

Shimmering wings beat hard and fast, lifting me over the park, taking me higher and higher into the twilight until the town below became a distant flicker of lights. But I didn't stop even when I lost sight of the houses.

I flew on across open countryside until I reached the coast, where the sea met the crumbling cliffs and shingle beaches. I looked down and saw a pier jutting out into the sea and a row of little fishing boats heading out towards the horizon. I flew on, with the night growing darker around me, following the meandering coastline, past inlets and harbours and amusement arcades, sandy beaches and rocky cliffs. Until there was sea below with a few scattered islands, and then nothing but water.

And still I flew, eyes fixed on the shining light of one brilliant star. At last a glimmer of morning light began to appear and a new colour filled the sky. And then I finally saw it. A wide open land, bare and rocky, surrounded by sea and cut through with glaciers. I swooped lower, looking down on red-hot craters and great gushing fountains of steam that blasted up from the earth below. A living breathing land of fire and ice, stretching on and on.

Now my wings beat even harder, as though something was pulling me onward.

In the distance, I saw an enormous volcano. Its silhouette loomed high into the sky. And it was a second before I realised it was erupting! Great shards of colour shot out of the top of the volcano and into the sky. A blaze of orange streaked across the crater and then red and fiery white. I'd only ever seen volcanoes erupting on television. But I wasn't afraid. I flew on. Until I realised something strange.

I was close to the volcano now, but it was just as cold as ever. The volcano couldn't be erupting after all. But then what was causing the sky to burn with those incredible colours?

Suddenly I felt a burning inside my belly. It burst through me and flames shot from my open mouth. I swooped lower and roared at the sight before me.

Because the volcano was erupting with DRAGONS!

Dragons of every conceivable size and colour were rising out of the crater of the volcano and soaring up into the sky. With another burst of flames I swooped in to join them, and as I dived and wheeled about my scales flickered from fiery red to azure blue, from crimson to blazing orange to deep purple, lime green, brilliant white and midnight black. And the flames I breathed into the air shone so brightly my eyes burned with the glare.

Dozens of dragons circled around me. I was becoming part of the amazing dance above the crater. I could hear the other dragons calling out, long sonorous notes. And I raised my head and answered them.

Finally the dragons settled on the rim of the crater and I flew down to join them. One after another, the colourful dragons approached and greeted me. They bent their massive heads forward and we crossed necks and let our heads rest there, as the rising sun warmed the air with its reddening glow.

When I finally opened my eyes Flicker was there curled up next to me, his heat warming me like a comforting hot water bottle. He was changing colours just as he always did, but the purring I thought I used to hear now sounded more like a rumbling sigh.

I think I knew deep down that keeping Flicker wasn't right. You know things in your heart sometimes, before your head is ready to listen. And sadly, right then, my head was definitely not listening.

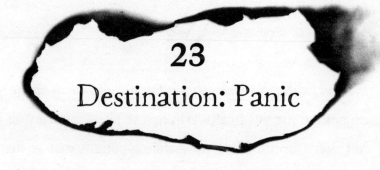

23
Destination: Panic

Usually when I feel upset or sad or worried about something, the superhero squad are on hand to cheer me up, or at least distract me. Ted brings out one of his weird and wonderful facts that startles your brain so much it can't be amazed *and* worry itself into knots at the same time. Like the fact that the average person has sixty-seven different species of bacteria living in their belly button. Or if you could look at the earth from sixty-five million light years away, you'd see dinosaurs. That sort of thing. It felt like a bit of me was missing without them there.

And of course there had always been Grandad. He didn't even need mind-boggling facts to make me feel better. When I pictured his twinkling smile, I knew I had to see him. After all, I could tell him the dragons had gone. I'd just have to skip over the teeny-tiny fact that not *all* the dragons had gone.

I found Mum in the kitchen, chatting away to the cockatoo. They were bobbing their heads up and down in unison.

'Can I go and see Grandad?' I asked.

Mum stopped mid-bob and turned to look at me. She sort of smiled and slowly nodded.

'I've been wanting to talk to you about Grandad,' she said. 'About how poorly he's been. And why he's still in hospital.'

'You mean his hip?' I asked. 'That's bound to take a bit of time to heal up.'

'Well, to be honest, love, it's a little bit more than the hip operation. Come and sit with me.' She sat down in the old squidgy armchair Grandad had given us and patted the armrest. I perched on it and she wrapped her arm around me.

'They wanted to know why he'd wobbled off the stool,' Mum said.

'Well, anyone can do that,' I said defensively. 'Especially Grandad, being so keen to get to Nana's tarts.'

Mum smiled. Another not-quite smile.

Grim's face suddenly flashed into my mind as I remembered what he'd said about Grandad's heart.

'That's true,' she said. 'But as it turns out he did have a funny turn again, and that's why he fell.'

I bit my lip as my heart shrivelled to the size of a crinkly dry raisin. So Grim had been right all along.

'But he'll be OK?' I asked quickly.

'Of course he will. He's a tough old boot, your grandad.'

My raisin heart stayed almost as small and tight as before.

Mum leaned over and gave me a squeeze. 'Is there anything else?'

Apart from the gigantinormous lie I'd told my best friends and the dragon sleeping upstairs who wasn't eating properly, there was actually. When I'd first found out about Grandad hurting his hip I was upset, of course I was. But there was a tiny  piece of me that was relieved that I wouldn't have to carry on lying to his face. And maybe even thought that I wouldn't have to rush into letting the dragons go. Now most of the dragons were gone anyway, I couldn't see my friends and I'd found out that Grandad was way more ill than I'd thought. I felt completely and utterly horrible. How could even an infinitesimal bit of me have felt relieved that Grandad was out of the way?

Part of me wanted Mum's squeeze to squeeze the whole terrible truth right out of me so she would see just what an awful person I was. I wriggled free and shook my head. It was bad enough worrying about Grandad, without making myself feel even worse.

Last time I had imagined the worst when I'd heard about Grandad. The worry had swelled to planet-size and exploded, but I had to remember the places my imagination went weren't always the right ones. Maybe I could give Destination: Panic a miss this time.

'So when can we go?' I asked.

'How about right now?' she said with a smile.

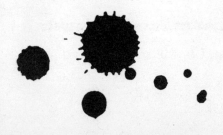

24
No Place like Home

Seeing Grandad in hospital wasn't as bad as I'd feared. Probably because of the huge ear-to-ear grin he gave me when I walked through the door.

'Chipstick!' he bellowed, and started waving madly as if I wouldn't be able to spot him. Which given there were only four beds in the ward wasn't exactly likely.

'You're a sight for sore eyes, Chipstick,' he said, still grinning. He patted the bed for me to sit down. 'Jelly?' he asked, offering me a spoon of wobbly green gloop.

I shook my head. Thanks to the TV shows Mum watched and my revved-up imagination, I realised I'd been imagining him lying pale and still on a hospital bed, with tubes and wires poking out of him. Now I was here, the relief at seeing him sitting up in his checked pyjamas, waving like a loon, started leaking out of me and I rubbed at my eyes, feeling a bit daft.

Grandad lowered the jelly and reached out his arm. I leaned in for a squeeze.

'Daft apeth,' he said softly, ramping up the squeeze till I thought my ribs would bust.

'Are you OK, Grandad?' I managed to squeak.

He let me go and waggled his finger at his hip as if telling it off.

'Soon as this fella sorts himself out I'll be right as rain,' he said.

'I mean, *really* OK?' I went on. 'Mum said it was your heart that made you fall.'

Grandad cleared his throat and turned his face into a more serious version of itself. For a moment he didn't say anything, like he was weighing up what to tell me.

'I know you, Chipstick. You're not really that daft. If I try and laugh this off, your old head'll start making up all sorts about what's going on now, won't it?'

I nodded, glad that he knew me well enough to see that I needed to hear the truth. Even if I didn't *want* to hear it.

'OK, here's the thing. My old heart did have a wobble. And that's why I took a tumble. Turns out all those times I've been huffing and puffing for breath in the garden lately, it's been trying to tell me something.'

I winced – I really should have been paying more attention. I should have been helping Grandad rather than spending all my time with the dragons.

'I'm sorry,' I muttered.

Grandad nudged me so I had to look up.

'What are you sorry for?'

I shrugged. Where should I start? Running him ragged when I was little? Not helping more in the garden? Lying to him about the dragons? Feeling relieved he'd not been at home to hold me to my promise to let them go?

'Come on, what's spinning round that head of yours?' he asked.

He carried on watching me, waiting for me to say something. His eyes were so intense I felt he was reading the thoughts in my head like an open book. Suddenly he let out a little '*hmm*', as though he'd turned the last page and finally figured it out.

'You know none of this is your fault, don't you, Chipstick? Not one little bit of it. You have *nothing* to feel sorry about. Got that?'

I gave a little nodling, which isn't really a proper nod at all but a tiny dip of the head. I still couldn't quite believe that, but I didn't want to upset him any more.

'And the great news,' Grandad said, giving me another nudge, 'is because of all the poking and prodding and checking they've done on account of this fall, they've figured out what the problem is. And they know just what to do to fix it.'

'Really?' I stammered. 'You're not just saying that?'

'Nope. I am definitely not just saying that. Things are going to be A-OK. OK?'

He looked me square in the eye and suddenly it was like the twinkle in there shot straight into my heart, a lightning bolt sent to blast all my worries to smithereens. I felt them starting to fizzle and fade.

I nodded, a proper nod this time, my shoulders sinking gratefully down from where they had attached themselves to my ears.

They shot straight up again though when Grandad whispered his next question.

'So, have you let those dragons go yet, like we agreed?'

The squirmy worms in my tummy woke up and started salsa dancing around my insides. Even though I could look him in the eye this time and say what he wanted to hear, I wasn't going to be telling the whole truth, was I?

I nodded, hoping that would be enough and that my crossed toes would make up for the bit of truth that was missing from the nod.

'Bet that was really hard,' he said, laying his hand on mine.

I nodded again, with more certainty this time. That was something I didn't have to lie about. It had been horrible watching Sunny, Crystal and Dodger fly away.

'It's for the best though,' Grandad said quietly. 'There's no place like home.' He shuffled up his bed and gave a little wince. 'Home is where the heart is, and mine definitely wants to get itself back there pronto.'

25
Superheroes Shouldn't Lie

On the way back from the hospital we stopped to pick Lolli up from nursery. She toddled towards us cradling a couple of cereal boxes splattered in paint with bits of tissue paper stuck all over them.

'For Tinkle,' she announced. And then whispered to me, 'Tinkle sad.'

I must have looked surprised because Lolli nodded seriously and said, 'All sad. Singsong gone.'

Now I thought of it, there was a definite absence of birds at home, apart from the cockatoo who didn't seem to be going anywhere. No stray emus, no inquisitive turkeys, no chicken strutting up and down on the breakfast table. Lolli was right. Tinkle had stopped singing.

'I'm sure that'll cheer her up,' I whispered back.

But I was suddenly aware of a nagging feeling pulling at me like Lolli when she was trying to get my attention. I shook the feeling off and stared out of the window.

But it got worse when we got home. Up in my room I found Flicker curled up on the windowsill staring out at the rain. Over the last week it seemed we'd had nothing but endless drizzle. When he saw me he lifted his head. His scales flickered red, glowing through the dull grey, and the twinkle returned to his

diamond eyes. But I couldn't help noticing the scales he had shed along the sill and across my desk.

Yes, I know, my heart was probably jumping up and down at this point, trying to get my head's attention. But my stubborn head was still refusing to listen.

I heard voices downstairs and just managed to scoop Flicker up and hide him under my bed when there came a tapping. The door swung open slowly and three heads peered round.

It wasn't the normal storming-in I was used to from Ted, Kat and Kai. But then nothing had been very normal since we'd let the dragons go. I'd hardly spoken to them, for one thing.

Ted gave me a nod and I got a wary 'Hiya' from Kai, but Kat hung back by the door, a worried look on her face.

'Your mum told us to come up,' Kai said, as if he needed to explain their arrival in my room.

I wasn't used to feeling awkward with my best friends. But I felt so bad about everything that had happened I didn't know what to say.

And then Kat stepped forward and I could see she was frowning back the tears.

'Look, I'm sorry, Tomas,' she said. 'I know you hate me right now, but please don't blame them. It was me who suggested letting the dragons go.'

I looked between the three of them, now shuffling uncomfortably. And I realised that they were feeling bad too. They'd thought I was avoiding them because I blamed them for losing Flicker. Great. Now I felt even worse.

'We all feel the same, Tomas,' said Kai. 'We all miss them. But I think we did the right thing.'

I winced inwardly as they waited for me to say something.

'It's fine,' I mumbled at last. 'Of course I don't blame you.'

They let out a collective sigh and Ted, relieved of his burden, jumped on my bed and started tucking into a packet of crisps. I bit my lip hoping Flicker wouldn't smell the vinegar. He loved salty crisps, and vinegar was something he couldn't resist. I silently begged him to stay hidden.

I noticed Kai following my gaze, which was fixed on the floor by the foot of my bed, and I hurriedly looked away.

'Glad that's sorted,' said Ted through a mouthful. 'Now, time to fill you in on that sneak Liam. We've been keeping our eyes on him and he's definitely up to something.'

'What's happened?' I asked, glad that Ted's expert crisp-eating skills meant he'd already demolished the lot, although the smell still lingered.

'Well, nothing. But he keeps disappearing.'

I frowned.

'Disappearing?'

'On a bus,' Ted added, as he carefully and

thoroughly licked each finger.

'Every day after school he gets on the Number 6 at the top of the road,' explained Kai.

'And tell him how sneaky he looks,' Kat said.

She apparently wasn't ready to believe I'd completely forgiven her yet and risk talking to me directly.

'We don't know what he's playing at, but what if he's gone and grown himself another dragon-fruit tree?' Kai went on.

'But like we said, it won't do him any good, will it?' I pointed out.

There was a moment's silence.

'But what if we're wrong?' Kat said, finally addressing me.

'What do you mean?'

'What if somehow he *has* managed to grow dragons?'

I was about to reply when Kai leaped off the bed shrieking. He clutched his foot, which had been dangling over the side.

'What's the matter?' Kat cried.

Kai jumped up and down, batting at his trouser leg, which we all suddenly realised was smoking. Everyone turned and looked at me. I felt my heart plummet through the floor and splat against the tiles in the kitchen.

Time slowed down like it does in films. I imagined Crystal's breath freezing everyone and me darting down to grab Flicker and hurry him safely into hiding. But Crystal was long gone. And time couldn't slow down long enough to stop Kat bending down and peering under the bed.

When her head reappeared it was more fiery red than any dragon's flame and her laser eyes bore right into me, sizzling any bravado I might have had to dust. Sitting on her hand was Flicker. He sent out another spray of sparks and fluttered up towards my shoulder.

Without saying a word, Kat turned, stormed out of the room and thundered down the stairs.

Kai and Ted stared at Flicker, now perched on my shoulder.

I could see Kai biting back angry words. In the end he unleashed a garbled shout and stomped out after Kat. Ted looked sadly from Kai's retreating back to me. Then his shoulders crumpled and he just shook his head sadly and followed the others.

I watched them go and thought of how Liam always called me ant-boy because I was small. Right then I felt smaller than any ant. I felt flea-sized and just as unwanted.

26
Some Grim Advice

The next few days were horrible, with stony glares from Kat and Kai, and sorrowful glances from a bewildered Ted. I'd lied to my best friends and been found out. I couldn't blame them for treating me like the last mouldy strawberry in the punnet that no one wants. And at home even Lolli was looking glum, after failing to cheer up Tinkle and bring her 'singsong' back.

Which is maybe why I started spending most of my free time in Grandad's garden. I couldn't do anything about the dragons leaving, or having upset Ted, Kat and

Kai, or about Grandad being in hospital. But I thought at least I could take a leaf out of Grim's book and make sure the garden was in a fit state for when Grandad got home. I busied myself with clearing rubbish, raking the hard earth, pulling out weeds, tidying the shed and cleaning all the tools.

Whenever I turned up Grim would poke his head over the fence from next door and give me a nod. A couple of times he even came over to help me drag the wheelbarrow about or bash away at the cloggy mud. I couldn't help wondering if I'd been wrong about him. He wasn't exactly the friendliest carrot in the bunch, but he hadn't really done anything to deserve all the scowls I'd launched his way over the past months.

I decided it might just be time to follow Grandad's example. He always said you could never know what was going on with people. They could have sat on a bee or be waiting for everyone to remember their birthday for all we know, he'd say. Maybe he was right and sometimes you just had to fight fire with friendliness.

Which is why when Grim next lived up to his name, for once I did things differently. He'd been muttering from the other side of the fence and, instead of hiding out of his way or jumping to the conclusion that he was cross and blaming me for something, I leaned over and, taking a steadying breath, I said:

'Er . . . Is everything OK?'

Grim looked as surprised by this question as I felt asking it. I thought for a minute he might turn beetroot and blast an angry bellow in my direction. But he actually rammed his spade into the ground and let out a sigh.

'Bloomin' mouse,' he said.

'Oh,' I replied sympathetically. 'Is it nibbling your lettuces again?'

For a second he looked at me like I was completely barmy. Then a flicker of the first smile I'd ever seen crossed his face.

'Computer mouse,' he said.

It wasn't the mouse's fault, of course. It was the computer programme that had crashed. The screen was frozen on the face of a young man. Grim had complained all the way up to the house about the 'dratted thing' not working and how he couldn't 'figure out how to get the blasted device to work for love nor money'. But in the end it didn't take me long to sort it for him.

He watched me as I tapped away, shaking his head.

'Guess I'm a bit out of touch with this stuff,' he said. 'I haven't a clue where to start.'

'It's OK,' I said. 'I can show you what I did if you like. It's dead useful and it's pretty simple.'

He rubbed his cheek, looking doubtful.

'I gave Grandad a few lessons last summer. He didn't think he'd pick it up either, but he did.'

Grim gave a little huff. 'So how is your grandad? Better, I hope?'

'He will be,' I said.

I smiled then, and he smiled back. A proper smile this time. And it made him look quite different.

As the screen woke up I couldn't help looking at the grinning young man.

'That's my son, Crispin,' Grim said. 'He's in Australia and I've been trying to make this thing work so I can talk to him and my granddaughter.'

I remembered Grandad telling me that Grim's wife had died. I couldn't help thinking it must be hard for him with his son so far away.

'Has he been there a long time?' I asked.

Grim nodded. 'I didn't want him to go, not one bit,' he said. 'Probably the only thing me and my Moll ever fought about.'

'She wanted him to go?' I asked, surprised.

'No, course she didn't,' Grim replied quietly. 'No more than I did. But Molly knew it was what he wanted and he needed to do it. "He'll be back," she said. And she was right, as usual. He's been there a few years now, met Tanika, that's his wife, and they've got a little girl now. But he knows where I am, and I know he'll come back one day. Maybe not to live, but to visit, I'm sure. When you love someone, you have to love them enough to let them go. Even if that's the hardest thing for you.'

I nodded. Somewhere inside it felt like a tight knot was loosening.

You know what, I think I'll stop calling him Grim here. Because his name's Jim. And he's not grim. And without even knowing it, he was the one to finally make my head catch up with what my heart had known all along.

That I needed to let Flicker go.

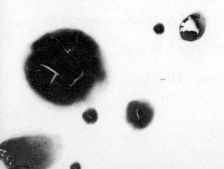

27
A Rare and Special Creature

Now that my head had finally caught up, things were looking pretty clear. For one thing, all the rain we'd been having suddenly made a lot more sense. I mean, what else is going to happen when a weather dragon is feeling sad? It also explained the dull and shedding scales and the fact he hadn't even been tempted out by the smell of Ted's vinegary crisps. It was horrible thinking that my keeping Flicker was what had made him so sad. I was beginning to feel like I was as bad as Liam.

But later, when Flicker curled up on my lap and shimmered his deep ruby red and blew his smoky breath across my hands, he didn't look sad at all.

I lay my hand on his back. 'I don't want you to leave, but I think you have to go home. It's for the best,' I whispered, remembering Grandad's words. Flicker gave a little rumble. He lifted his head and I felt his diamond eyes looking right into my heart.

There were two more things that were crystal clear. One was that I needed to talk to Lolli, and the second was that I had to find out what Liam was up to. I was dreading telling Lolli that Tinkle needed to go. But it turned out that, as usual, Lolli knew far more than you'd expect from a three-year-old.

The next morning she sneaked into my room before Mum and Dad were awake. Without saying anything she climbed up onto my bed and settled Tinkle next to Flicker. Then she shoved a small plastic suitcase into my ribs. I sat up, rubbing my side.

'Ow! What's up, Lollibob?' I whispered.

Carefully she unlatched the case and I saw what was inside. A splodge of hairy blue rock-hard icing, a fairy finger puppet and a crumpled piece of sugar paper with her little handprint on it.

'Tinkle go bye-bye,' she said, in the kind of voice that would make Cruella de Vil want to give her her own puppy. Talk about pulling at your heart strings – she'd just yanked mine clean out.

I nodded. Then gave a feeble smile and a double thumbs up. I hoped Liam would be this good about giving up his dragon. Somehow I very much doubted it though.

After I led Lolli back to her room, I reached under my pillow and pulled out Elvi's journal. Without Kat, Kai and Ted, it felt like Elvi was the only one I could talk to – and I wasn't even really talking to her, just listening. But it made me feel less lonely somehow. She must have felt something similar, leaving Arturo behind knowing that, once she was back home, the secret of the dragons would be hers alone.

My fingers flicked through the pages until a sketch of a campfire in one of the early entries caught my eye.

It was always round the campfire that Elvi and Arturo revealed the most. I began to read.

Tonight one of the men asked what happened to this great city of ours. He thinks we are quite mad to seek a city that is probably just a myth. This part of the story is where Arturo always prods the fire and grows a little quiet.

With the dragons always leaving, it was important for the people to hatch new dragons. For this to happen they knew they must do their utmost to care for the tree. Because for a long, long time there was only one tree that bore dragons.

And then a dragon hatched that had the power to breathe life into seeds. This was a rare and special creature. One in a hundred thousand. Maybe even one in a million.

My skin tingled. I'd been right! There *was* a special dragon that had breathed life into the dragon-fruit tree. One that turned the normal fruits into ones that glowed and hatched dragons.

> *People rejoiced. Believing their problems were solved. That dragons would live within the forest forever now. With so many activated dragon-fruit trees, their troubles would be over.*
>
> *It meant the dragons had a future. And then so did the people. But it also brought disaster.*

Flicker blew a warming breath across my hand, which I saw was now shaking. But even with that the room felt suddenly cold.

> *This dragon made the land more fertile than it had ever been. But a rival to the ruling emperor entrapped the dragon. He didn't want this dragon soaring to the stars. He could see it bringing him great wealth and even greater power.*
>
> *But there is no controlling a dragon.*

> *It grew fast and it grew big. And the green flames that spurted from its belly were too powerful. They razed the land, annihilating the crops and trees, and burned the great city to dust.*

As my eyes fell on those last words it was like a burst of flame rocketed through me. A dragon that made things grow. A dragon with fiery green breath. A dragon just like Liam's!

I looked at Flicker. He was hovering in front of me now, shimmering electric orange, his tail cracking sparks against the headboard of the bed.

If I was right and Liam really did have an activator dragon, then things were even worse than we'd thought. He could be out there right now, hatching as many dragons as he liked. Every day that dragon stayed in our village was a day too long. It could destroy everything!

28
Undercover

For a moment I thought I should try to appeal to Liam's better side to persuade him to let the dragon go. But then I remembered he didn't have one. Really the only option was to be as sneaky as he was. I wished the superhero squad were with me. But after what I'd done, I couldn't expect them to come to the rescue – not this time. It was up to me.

Thanks to Ted telling me about Liam getting on the Number 6 bus after school every day, it wasn't too hard to find him. Luckily the bus stop nearest to his house was just before a junction. This meant I could keep out of sight till the last minute. I peered round the hedge on the corner of the street and saw him waiting. He was looking the other way, up the street, obviously looking out for the bus. He had a bag slung over his shoulder, and by the way he was leaning I could tell it was quite heavy. And he kept hugging it close to him, like I was doing with mine in fact, aware of Flicker and Tinkle curled up inside. As I watched, his bag shook slightly. Yup! It was pretty clear it wasn't just his lunch in there. After a few minutes a double-decker bus appeared at the top of the road and rattled its way down towards the bus stop.

Now, obviously I couldn't just run out and jump on. I needed to stay undercover to see where he was going. Hopefully it was somewhere a bit less public because, let's face it, trying to wrestle a dragon off him on a bus that was full of people wasn't really an option. I watched him pay the driver and waited, willing him to head upstairs. If he stayed on the lower deck I doubted my expert disguise of Dad's fishing hat and Mum's knitted scarf would really stand up.

The bus was crowded, but through the window I could see that there was a spare seat, next to a woman holding a tiny dog. It was wearing what looked like a woolly jumper and had its nose pressed against the glass. Liam obviously decided to take his chances upstairs. As soon as his foot hit the second step and his head had disappeared from sight I bolted towards the bus stop.

It was no good though. I wasn't going to make it. I could hear the driver revving the engine. He hit the button and the doors began to close just as I reached the curb. In a panic I grabbed my scarf, lunged forwards and whirled it through the narrowing gap. The doors closed on it with a clunk. As the bus lurched into motion I clung to the other end. Just for a second there I was running alongside the bus, gripping my scarf. I could see one of the passengers waving at me to let go and another man shouting to the driver.

By the time the driver stopped the bus and opened the doors I had a feeling my career as an undercover agent was well and truly over.

'What the dickens are you playing at?' said the driver crossly as I staggered up the steps.

'Sorry,' I panted, trying to think quickly and acutely aware of the many eyes fixed on me. 'I was meeting a mate. He just went upstairs and I didn't want to miss him.' I paused to give him a weak smile. 'Same fare as him, please.' I held out a trembling handful of loose change, desperately hoping it was enough.

The driver grumbled something and picked out some coins.

'Er . . . Where is it I'm going?' I asked.

The driver looked at me and frowned even more. I must have sounded like a total muppet. I mean, who gets on a bus and has no idea where they're even going?

'Botanic garden,' he barked. 'Although if you don't leave me in peace sharpish, you'll be going nowhere.'

The botanic garden? The words hit me like a punch in the stomach, knocking the air right out of me. What better place to find – or grow – an exotic plant? I didn't need to be a genius to work out that Liam must have got himself another dragon-fruit tree. I staggered as the bus moved forward.

I shuffled down to the seat next to the lady with the miniature dog.

'Your friend is up there,' she said, smiling, and pointed to the steps leading upstairs.

'That's OK,' I said awkwardly. And then with a total brain-wave I added, 'I don't like heights.'

I sank down into the seat, cradling my coat and the bag with Flicker and Tinkle inside, my head full of Liam and what I would find in the botanic garden. The little dog wriggled across the woman's lap and started whining. His pointy ears pricked up and he had his eyes fixed on my bag. He started straining to get a closer look, his little sniffs getting more urgent. Then the

whining got louder and several people started tutting about animals on buses.

The woman looked at me again, a mix of embarrassment and crossness colouring her face. I shrank down lower, cradling the bag as it began to shift about. I imagined Flicker's head popping out and sending a fiery sneeze at the inquisitive dog. People were definitely staring in our direction now. But if they thought a boy in a fishing hat and purple knitted scarf clutching a wriggling bag was weird, wait till they found out they were traveling with two dragons. Three, if you counted the one I was pretty sure was upstairs.

I didn't appear any less weird when we reached the stop for the botanic garden. As Liam came down the stairs I dived to the floor and started scrabbling under the seat in an attempt to hide. The now overexcited dog jumped down after me, seizing his chance to get his nose in my bag. He was so alarmed by what was inside that he was baring his teeth. And those teeth looked like sharp little needles, I can tell you.

A shout came from the front of the bus and I looked up to see the driver leaning round from his cab up front.

'Oi!' he said again. And pointed at Liam, who was already off the bus and scurrying down the street.

'I'm not having any more last-minute dives for the door. Look lively, will you?'

Casting an apologetic look at the woman, whose dog had thankfully been diverted by another passenger's bag of shopping, I raced off the bus. Somehow I didn't think I'd be catching the Number 6 again in a hurry.

29
Into the Rainforest

I hurried after Liam, keeping out of sight. The gates of the botanic garden were already locked, but this didn't seem to bother him. I saw him take a quick look around and then wriggle through a gap between the hedge and the metal railing. He pulled his bag after him and disappeared into the undergrowth on the other side. This obviously wasn't his first time sneaking in.

It was getting late and the weather wasn't helping much. I can't say I relished the idea of creeping round the huge park-like garden on my own in the dark. But I'd be doing just that if I didn't follow Liam quickly to see exactly where he was heading.

I pushed my way through the same gap and battled the thorny stems until I emerged covered in damp leaves. Liam was jogging away down the path, brushing bits of hedge out of his hair. Mum and Dad brought us to the botanic garden quite a lot and I knew bits of it well, but there were gloomy edges and shadowy corners that didn't seem quite as inviting to explore in the dark. I reached into my bag and lifted out Flicker and Tinkle, glad that they were here with me. I couldn't help noticing the scales left in the bottom of the rucksack. Flicker had been shedding more than ever in the last few days. I settled a dragon on each shoulder and then followed Liam.

He was hurrying down the path, past the pond and the magnolia trees and straight on towards the glasshouses.

I remembered the last time we'd visited, the sweltering wall of heat that had met us as we left the cooler alpine room with its delicate flowers and opened the door into the dangly tangled vines of the rainforest area. And then how we had gasped in relief as we finally reached the less intense heat beyond, where huge palms grew.

Peering through the glass doors I could see that it was into the humid rainforest room that Liam was now creeping.

I waited for him to disappear inside and then turned the handle of the main door and pushed, wincing as it creaked slightly. The glass-roofed corridor I found myself in was lined with exotic plants, their heady scent filling the air. I passed a plant with broad leaves and strange bird-head flowers, edging away from the rolled-up pointed green of the beak, with its orange and purple petals sprouting like a plume of feathers. They watched me beadily as I went past.

Crouching low, I saw Liam on the other side of the glass. He stepped off the path and pushed his way past the giant fronds of a prehistoric-looking fern. I held back a moment and then followed him inside.

The damp heat clung to me as soon as I entered. Thick rope-like vines hung down through glossy leaves as big as dinner plates, and vast pitcher plants in bright reds and yellows leaned towards me, like they could taste me in the air. It really was like being transported to a tropical rainforest, and I couldn't help thinking of Elvi and Arturo pushing their way through the undergrowth.

I carried on and came to a spiralling iron staircase with a lopsided sign reading 'Private'. It was draped with frilly tendrils and disappeared among the vegetation above. But looking up I could see a balcony running around the top of the glasshouse walls.

It was getting harder to breathe in the stuffy tropical air, although that didn't seem to bother Flicker and Tinkle, who left my shoulders and flitted between the red pompom flowers of a low-hanging tree.

Finally the air changed a little and so did the plants. Ahead of me I heard Liam yelp and wondered if he had caught himself on one of the many vicious thorns I was starting to pick my way past.

Then I heard his footsteps stop. Ducking out of sight

behind a plant with huge fern-like leaves, I sneaked a look.

He was kneeling on the ground in front of a tree. Not just any tree. A tree with a knobbly, hairy trunk. With long spiky green leaves that hung down in a familiar sprouty mop-top. And vivid tendrils like bursts of flame.

I watched, open-mouthed, as he reached up to touch a spiky dragon fruit nestled on one of the tendrils.

Carefully he opened his bag and lifted out the grey dragon. He held it under one arm and then cupped the dragon fruit in the other hand.

The dragon let out a green blast. And then another. And another. Until the dragon fruit began to glow.

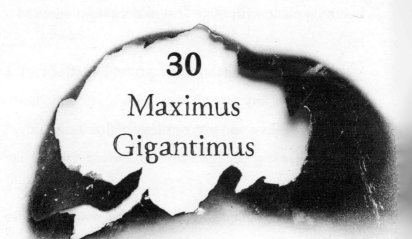

30
Maximus Gigantimus

I couldn't take my eyes off the glowing dragon fruit. I stepped closer but felt my foot slip in something mushy, I looked down and saw the pulpy remains of a dragon fruit. And then a smell of fish and burnt toast wafted towards me.

Suddenly a shape zipped down from above. I ducked as a blue and yellow dragon with orange spikes flew straight at me. It let out a smoky belch and dropped another rank-smelling poo. I stumbled out of its path, tripped on a root and launched forward. Liam spun round with the dragon fruit now loose in his hand, as I fell sprawling at his feet.

'What do you think you're doing?' I cried, no longer caring that my great attempt at sneaking up on him had failed. I scrambled to my feet and glared at him.

He looked too stunned to speak. I'd obviously been pretty good at the whole undercover thing after all.

'Well?' I snapped.

Before he could answer, the fruit he was holding glowed brighter and the next second it burst. Liam lunged to catch the little dragon before it fell to the ground. He cradled it in his hands, staring at the turquoise dragon with its two-pronged tail that flicked in opposing directions. I was still glaring at him.

'They're all so different,' he said quietly.

This wasn't the reaction I was expecting. I had been preparing myself for a shove or a shout or the old faithful, 'Bog off, Whiffy.' So for a second I was a bit taken aback.

I gathered my thoughts. 'You have no idea what you're doing,' I said. 'You have to stop this.'

'*I* haven't done anything,' said Liam simply. 'Maxi has.'

'Maxi?'

'My dragon. Maximus Gigantimus,' Liam said. Then he shrugged. 'But he's just Maxi really.'

I looked at the grey dragon, who had curled himself around Liam's foot. Liam wiped his hands on his trousers, trying to remove the sticky pulp from the burst fruit.

'I heard you outside class,' he said.

I must have sneered, because he jumped in with a feeble defence.

'Look, you were the ones blabbing about stuff. I couldn't help being there. I wasn't spying on you.'

'For once,' I muttered. But he gave me a look, as if to say 'And who's just been spying on me?'

'So?' I grumbled.

'So you were talking about that woman, Elvi, and the tree. Kat said maybe the legend you'd read was wrong and that dragons breathed on the fruit. And that's how a dragon-fruit tree became active. But you said it yourself, maybe it took a special dragon.'

We both looked down at the dragon at Liam's feet,

who was now glowing a bright green. Liam gave a little cough like he was clearing the words out of his throat.

'I think Maxi's pretty special,' he said.

Part of me was glad that Liam seemed to have finally got that. At least Kat could stop worrying about him not treating his dragon with due care and respect and all that. But he had more to say.

'After I heard what you said I went looking for one of the fruits. I thought I could get Maxi to grow a tree fast and then breathe on it. I wanted to see if I was right. I mean, his breath makes stuff grow super-big and super-fast. You've seen that too. But maybe it would do more than that. But it turns out dragon fruits aren't easy to find. No one even seemed to know what they were. But then I found out there was a tree here in the botanic garden. I didn't need to grow one. I figured it was worth a shot. I wanted to find out exactly what Maxi could do.'

I snorted. Liam had no idea what Maxi was capable of – but I was about to fill him in on that.

'This is serious, Liam. Maxi is special, you're right. He's an "activator" dragon and they are rare. *Really* rare. But they're also dangerous if they're kept too long. It's happened before. Some power-crazy muppet thought he could use a dragon like Maxi to become the next emperor of the Hidden City – and instead he ended up destroying everything.'

Liam didn't even look like he was listening; he was looking around the glasshouse, scanning the vines and leaves. I wanted to reach out, grab him and shake some sense into him.

Suddenly there was a flash of scarlet and then silver. And two dragons darted out from behind the foliage. They circled us for a moment and then flew up towards the roof.

'Liam . . .' I said warily, 'how many dragons have you grown?'

'Enough,' he said gruffly.

'Enough to do what exactly?'

31
Liam's Big Secret

Before he could answer, six . . . seven . . . no, at least ten dragons burst out of the tangle of plants and started flitting around us. And then more and more and more. There must have been forty dragons circling the glasshouse.

'What have you done?' I yelled. 'They're going to destroy this place.'

I was surprised the whole glasshouse hadn't exploded from the amount of poo this lot must have produced. But then I realised that maybe this was the one place it would be OK. It was so humid that the poo probably never dried out enough to detonate. That was one good thing anyway. But, let's face it, dealing with forty-plus dragons was not exactly going to be a walk in the park.

'We've got to get them out of here,' I said. 'Before they go and set fire to everything.'

'They won't,' Liam said matter-of-factly.

'How do you know that?'

'Well, they haven't so far. And it's their home – why would they destroy it?'

'*This* isn't their home,' I shouted. '*This* is a greenhouse.'

Frustration got the better of me and I snapped. 'Why are you doing this? You can't keep this secret. What'll happen when people find out? Or maybe that's what you want. It is, isn't it? You just want to tell everyone, "Hey, I'm Liam. I'm the King of Dragons." Just like the show-off you are.'

Liam frowned and I stepped back, braced for the shove I was sure was coming this time.

'Shut up,' he shouted. 'That's not it.'

'Well, why *have* you done it?'

He opened his mouth to speak and then closed it again. His lips went really thin like he was pinching back the words.

'Well?' I snarled.

'Maxi's my friend,' Liam muttered at last. And then added, 'He's the only one who's ever stuck around.'

He stared right at me and I remembered my mum telling me how we had once been friends. Until we'd gone to school, that was. And I'd had Ted there. Ted, who I'd known all my life. And who found it easy to go over to people like Kat and Kai, making friends for us both. Making us a little band of four.

'It's all right for you and the rest of your little gang. "Hey, look at us – we're the superhero squad." I know I'm not cool like Jay or cute like Bea,' Liam said. 'I didn't do this to show off. I did it because . . .'

Maxi raised his head and started nibbling on Liam's trouser leg. Liam reached down to touch the dragon's head.

'Because I wanted some more,' he growled.

'More what?' I cried.

For a second we both just looked at each other, and then he gave a little sigh.

'Friends,' Liam said simply. 'I wanted some more friends, all right? Happy now?'

I felt myself shrinking down to ant-size.

And not because Liam was being mean.

But because I suddenly knew exactly how he felt.

Ever since I'd lied to Ted, Kat and Kai, I'd been on my

own. And it didn't feel nice. Not nice at all.

'But you can't keep them,' I said quietly.

'Why not?' Liam replied, full of bluster now. 'I'm not hurting them and they aren't hurting me.' He straightened and squared up to me and I remembered his ability to go properly Hulk. 'So you can shove off and leave us alone.'

'But that's just it – you are,' I said, standing my ground. 'Just keeping them like this *is* hurting them.' And I thought again of Flicker's dull scales. I reached down towards his dragon, realising this might be my one and only chance to snatch him away.

'No!' Liam spat, grabbing Maxi before I could get to him. Convinced he was going to hurt me this time for sure, I backed away and fell, scraping my hands on the rocky ground. Ahead, something large and green burst through the foliage towards us.

'Step away from the dragon!' it yelled.

32
Trust the
Superhero Squad

Kat launched herself at Liam and he too stumbled back. Behind her came Kai, breathless and holding his side. Ted followed, looking red-faced.

'Since when did you get so fast?' he groaned. 'You were meant to wait for us, you know.'

I looked at the three of them. It was so good to see them that I just couldn't help grinning. I wasn't going to have to handle Liam and a room full of dragons by myself after all. Ted grinned back.

'You didn't think we'd let you face the King of Trouble all on your own, did you?' he said.

'How did you even know I was here?' I asked.

'Give us *some* credit,' Kai said.

'You mean, give *me* some credit,' Kat said. 'Since I was the one who figured out where Liam was heading every day. It was in Elvi's diary. She gave the second tree to the head gardener here. She seemed to think it was the best place, until she could work out why it never grew dragons. I thought Liam must have found out there was one here.'

'But it was me who saw you jump on that bus,' Kai said, 'and went back for the others. It looked like you were trying to lasso it with your scarf!'

Kat was pulling Liam roughly to his feet and looked ready to throttle him. But she didn't get a chance because Maxi, alarmed at this attack, let out a fiery jet of green. The prickly-edged leaves next to Kat ballooned in size. She staggered out of the way, dropping Liam's arm.

'Hey,' she shouted, rubbing her leg where the prickles had speared her. 'That hurt.'

But the dragon was in no mood to let her off so lightly. It sent more jets into the foliage. Immediately plants started super-sizing every which way. The vines thickened like enormous snakes, and leaves that were already big swelled to the size of umbrellas. We pushed our way out on to the path away from the creaking groans of the growing jungle. And then shrieked as we saw the now gigantinormous jaws of a Venus flytrap. It could have swallowed all four of us and still had room for dessert.

All the commotion was getting the other dragons nosy. Suddenly five or six zipped down to join in.

'Flaming fiery fiasco,' Kat yelled. 'Liam's got himself a dragon army!'

'I knew he was up to no good,' Kai growled.

'Not again,' moaned

Ted, desperately wiping runny dragon poo off his arm. 'It better not explode. This jacket's brand new. Mum'll go Vesuvius on me.'

Shielding themselves from the dragons, who had started sending sparks and, in some cases, fiery blasts in their direction, Kat and Kai grabbed Liam.

'What have you done?' they bellowed at him. Kat looked ready to wrestle him to the ground.

'Stop,' I said.

They looked at me like I'd gone mad. And I couldn't blame them. I'd been on the end of Liam's mean comments enough times to know how back to front me sticking up for him sounded. But I'd learned something else now. Grandad was right – you don't always know what's going on with people. Liam hadn't sat on a bumble bee, and everyone hadn't forgotten his birthday, as far as I knew, but he had felt left out from the moment he'd got to school. And if I was being honest, that was partly our fault. Even recently when he'd tried to talk to me, like at Lolli's party, it'd been

215

me who had slammed the door – quite literally – in his face.

'That's not what he was doing,' I said.

Liam flushed red and glared at me. I wondered if he was regretting being quite so honest. After all, I had the power here to shrink him down to amoeba-size, let alone ant-size. All I had to do was christen him Liam 'No Mates' Sawston. I tried to give him my most reassuring look.

'Trust me,' I said, my words meant for him as much as the others, 'he's looking after them.'

I could tell they still weren't convinced. It looked like Liam wasn't the only one not sure whether to trust me. I hadn't exactly earned the superhero squad's trust back yet. I'd have to hope the practicalities would win out.

'We need his help to let them go. He's the only one Maxi will listen to.'

'Who on earth is Maxi?' Kai said.

'His dragon. The one who could turn our whole

village into the rainforest if he carries on super-sizing everything in here.'

Kat's expression changed; the laser beams were retracting. I wondered if the fact that Liam had given his dragon a name had worked in his favour.

'He's not going to let them go,' said Ted. 'We heard him say as much.'

'Yes, he is,' I said. 'Aren't you, Liam?' I looked him straight in the eye. I needed to make him understand.

'I know how cool it is to have a dragon,' I continued. 'I got there first, remember? But we're going to let them go. OK? They all need to go home. And that includes Maxi. He's special. He's an activator dragon, and we need to keep him safe. Elvi hatched dragons for years without finding one of those. Who knows when another one will come along. The dragons need him. Without him, they might not have a future. I was wrong to keep Flicker.'

I kept his gaze.

'I was wrong about a lot of stuff.'

Everything was riding on Liam believing me and agreeing. If he didn't join us, then we had no chance against Maxi's super-sizing jets.

Liam dipped his head in a tiny, barely noticeable nod. Hardly even a nodling. But I'd seen it, and a sigh of relief burst out of me. I grinned like a lunatic as Liam lifted his hands to his mouth. Cupping them in front of his lips, he made a hooting noise. Maxi stopped in mid-blast and flew down towards us.

'Right, let's send this lot home,' I said.

33
Tinkle, Tinkle, You Little Star

Letting the dragons go wasn't going to be easy. The excitement of the super-sizing had sent them into a frenzy. In the jungle of the greenhouse we could hardly keep them in sight, let alone catch them. They darted around us, sending out sparks that scorched leaves and frazzled flowers. I just hoped Liam was right and everything didn't actually go up in flames.

I noticed that Kat had spotted Tinkle and Flicker though. She smiled as the little silver dragon fluttered down and settled on her hand while Flicker circled her head. I hoped seeing them wouldn't remind her how mad she'd been at me for lying.

But she turned the smile towards me.

'We can do what we did last time,' she said. 'They'll follow her song.'

'Absolutely,' I said, feeling relief swirl around my chest like Lolli's multi-coloured windmill from the garden twirling in the breeze. 'That's a great idea.'

Maybe this wasn't going to be so hard after all.

'We need to open one of the skylights,' I said. 'That way they can just fly up and out and we won't risk losing any on the way through the rest of the glasshouse.'

'How are we meant to do that?' Ted asked. 'We can't get up that high.'

'We don't need to,' I said. 'There was a handle back there. You wind it and the skylight opens.'

I raced towards the handle, followed by everyone else. I started winding it madly, eyes fixed on the roof. One of the panes opened a tiny crack and there was a cheer from Kai and Ted.

'Keep going,' Kat said, still cradling Tinkle.

But suddenly there was a juddering crunch and the handle came off in my hand. I held it up to show the others.

'What now?' I groaned.

'I know they're small, but I don't think even the newly hatched ones will get through that gap,' Kat said.

'Come on,' said Liam, pulling at my arm.

He dragged me away from the others towards the half-hidden spiral staircase. The next second he had leaped over the sign saying 'Private' and was legging it up towards the balcony. I followed as the others watched nervously.

It was high up there. *Really* high. We were face to face with the tops of the broad-leaved trees, moving through the canopy. The floor of the balcony was like a grid so water from the humid air didn't pool. But it meant we could see right down through the gaps in the foliage to the ground. My heart trampolined up

into my mouth every time I shot a glance downwards. I gripped the railings. But Liam hurried on.

When I caught up with him, he was staring up at the jammed skylight.

'If I can get onto that ledge that runs round the wall, I think I can pull myself up and reach it,' he said. 'I just need you to give me a leg-up.'

There was no 'just' about it. I could see that there was a gap between the balcony and the wall. If Liam slipped he'd fall straight down, all the way to the ground far below.

'Down there you were asking me to trust you,' he said. 'Thanks, by the way, for not, you know, blabbing about my lack of friends.'

I nodded. 'I'm sorry. We didn't exactly go out of our way to let you join in. That's not what mates are meant to do. And we *were* mates once.'

Liam shrugged. 'That's OK. I guess I didn't take it very well.'

'Nah, not *very* well,' I laughed, remembering all the times he had been a total pain.

'Well, now you can trust me too,' Liam said. 'I can climb stuff. I'm good at it. I can do this.'

'All right,' I said. 'You're on.'

Ted appeared at the top of the staircase just as I linked my fingers, and Liam stood on my joined hands. I started heaving him upwards. He scrabbled to find fingerholds on the wall.

'Steady on, Tomas,' Ted cried. 'I know he's a pain, but I don't think he deserves to plunge head first into a rabid Venus flytrap.'

It must have looked like I was trying to wrestle Liam off the balcony. I gave a final heave as Liam lunged for the ledge.

'Don't worry,' I said to Ted. 'We're on the same side now, remember?'

We looked up at Liam who had both feet on the ledge and was now reaching up to the roof. There was a rusty creak and a groan as he managed to push the skylight open. He'd done it!

Below I heard Kat and Kai cheer, and then Kat lowered her head to Tinkle and whispered something.

The little dragon rose into the air and began to sing. All around, the dragons stopped their crazed dive-bombing and fire-sparking. Even Maxi stopped blasting out his super-sizing green jets. Just like on the day of Lolli's party, I felt the whole atmosphere calming down as the music drifted and soothed.

One by one they followed the song and Tinkle led them up towards the open skylight and the blackness beyond.

34
A Diamond Is Forever

Liam's hand reached out to touch Maxi, his fingers skimming the lime green underside of the dragon's wings as he flew by. Now only Flicker remained and he fluttered along by me as we rushed out of the glasshouse to watch the others leaving, little darting flecks of colour in the stormy night sky. The stormy – and cloudy – night sky.

'Oh no!' I cried. 'There are no stars again.'

'Can Flicker clear the clouds?' Kat asked.

He flew down and rested on my shoulder.

'I hope so,' I said. But I looked nervously up at the brooding sky. This storm had been brewing all day. It felt like a lot to ask of the little dragon.

Flicker wrapped his tail around my neck and rested his head against my ear, blowing his warm breath right into the heart of me.

Before I could speak I felt his claws release and he launched up into the air. He began to spin round and round, just like he had in Grandad's garden. I smiled. He'd known what I needed him to do, without my even asking. But this storm was a giant and the air was heavy with its thunderous voice. Would it be too much for the little dragon? On and on he spun, getting faster and faster, brighter and brighter.

He seemed to be pulling the storm in, drawing it towards him as he soared higher and higher. Up there he shone like a diamond in the sky. Finally the heavy clouds of the storm began to clear.

The others cheered as dragons started rising up in spirals, heading towards the now visible North Star. But, as I kept my eyes locked on Flicker, I could only gasp.

The little dragon had finally stopped spinning. He was tumbling. Down, down, down. Like a falling star.

I sprinted towards the open lawn, arms outstretched. If I could just reach him, if I could just hold on to him, then everything was going to be OK. But as he landed in my hands I knew that wasn't true.

Because the diamond light had faded. Flicker's eyes had closed.

Ted, Kat, Kai and Liam, who'd chased across the lawn with me, now stopped as I held the little dragon to my chest.

I felt Ted put a hand on my arm. And I thought I heard Kat's voice. But I was somewhere far away. Flying on the back of my dragon. Through a rain of tears.

'What have I done?' I whispered.

'This isn't your fault,' Kat said.

'It is!' I cried. 'I should have let him go with the others in the first place.'

'But he could have gone any time,' she said softly. 'He could have followed the others that first day in the garden. But he didn't. He chose to stay with you.'

'I know,' I said desperately. 'But that's only because he knew I didn't want him to go. Even when I told him he should, I still didn't *want* him to, not really. He must have known that.'

'And now?'

'Now it's too late.'

Tinkle fluttered down and perched on my arm. I should have known she wouldn't leave without Flicker. She laid her head across his neck. But Flicker didn't move. And this time his scales didn't change colour to match her silvery blue. She nudged him with her snout as if trying to wake him.

When he didn't stir, she looked up and began to sing. A haunting, drifting song that rose into the air, taking my heart with it.

Another dragon flew towards us. Liam pointed and cried, 'Maxi!'

The plump grey dragon puffed up, and his wings and spines shone a vivid green. His eyes were fixed on Flicker. By the time he reached us, he was pulsing as if he was radioactive. He flew close to Flicker, still lying in my hands, and opened his mouth. But instead of the usual steady green blast the breath that came from the dragon seemed to flicker through all the shades of green imaginable. Emerald, forest, olive, jade, lime, sea, neon and spring. The air around us shimmered with the light.

Like a mini aurora borealis. All of us stood, wrapped in the song and the green glow of the dragon's breath.

And then it happened. I felt my hands grow warm. A tingling spread up my arms. And Flicker's scaly belly nudged against my fingers as he took a breath.

His head lifted and I found myself staring into two diamond eyes that seemed to see right into the heart of me. And for the second time since Flicker had arrived, I felt like a firework display was going off inside me. Only this time the display was so huge it was like it was made of shooting stars.

'It's time to go,' I whispered. And this time I meant it.

I lifted him up in my hands till we were nose to snout. His tail curled round and tickled my ear. And as I whispered my goodbyes his scales flickered gold, lighting up my face. I felt his claws tighten on my palms as he prepared to launch and braced myself for the weightless feeling as he left my hands and rose into the air with Tinkle and Maxi.

I stood with Ted, Kat, Kai and Liam, and watched him fly higher and higher into the inky sky, a flicker of sparks lighting his path. I felt the cold of the night bite into me, as the fiery warmth of the little dragon disappeared forever.

Afterwards – And You Thought It Was All Over?

At last I know *for sure* that I did the right thing! You're not going to believe what has just happened. You're really not!

So it's been six months since I watched Flicker fly up into the sky, knowing I'd never see him again. Six months of missing him every single day. I can't write this fast enough. But I need to slow down and make sure I don't miss one bit of it. Because, believe me, you're going to want to hear this. Boy, are you going to want to hear this!

I'd just ambled back from tea with Nana and another stint in the garden with Grandad. Now he'd recovered from his hip operation and they'd sorted out the right type of pills to keep his heart happy, he was back to his usual twinkly self.

I turned back to see him still standing across the park, waiting till I gave him the 'I'm OK' wave. Well, I say 'wave'. It had started off with us holding one hand up, but over time it's developed into a pretty elaborate series of arm flagging, head flicks and leg kicks and even the odd twirl from Grandad. I laughed and gave a final bow before hurrying on home.

When I got inside I was met by an avalanche of sound. Screeches, yowls, howls and a rather disturbing squealing blasted out from the living room. With my hands over my ears I peered in. Dad had set up his keyboards and was in full swing, playing and singing his latest tunes to Mum, who was jumping around the room grinning and twirling her arms like a helicopter about to take off. She wasn't the only one enjoying the show, judging by the sounds the rest of the audience were making. And by audience I mean the cockatoo flapping overhead, the St Bernard stretched out on the sofa, the four cats – none of whom were Tomtom – and the little piglet. It was no wonder my parents hadn't ever noticed there were two dragons in the house!

I gave them a wave and headed up to my bedroom.

I could hear Lolli chattering away, pausing every so often to make murmurs of agreement as she stopped to hear the opinion of one of her cuddly toys. After all the digging Grandad had got me to do, and stuffed full of Nana's steamed jam sponge and custard, I fell onto my bed and was asleep before I'd even got undressed.

When I opened my eyes it was dark and a sticky hand was smooshing my face.

'Flickaflickaflickaflickaflicka,' Lolli babbled, the words blurring as they fell over themselves to get out of her mouth. She started pulling on my sleeve, trying to drag me out of bed.

I groaned and swung my legs out. 'It's OK, Lolli. Time to sleep. I'll tuck you in,' I yawned. But she stepped out of my reach.

'MewannaFlicka,' she insisted.

At first I thought she was just upset again. However grown-up she'd been about letting Tinkle and Flicker go, every so often the reality of not having a dragon in her pocket hit home.

'MewannaFlicka,' she said again, and pulled even harder at my arm. Then she pointed at the curtains.

As I rubbed the sleep from my eyes and looked at her properly, I suddenly realised she wasn't upset. She was just really super-excited.

I looked from her eager face to the window and she nodded, her little head bobbing up and down as she jiggled on the spot. I stepped forward, pulled back the curtain and peered out into the garden. And my mouth did that cartoon jaw-dropping thing. Lolli giggled and clapped her hands.

Because right there, filling up most of our small back garden, was a dragon. An enormous, glorious, shimmering dragon. It stretched its neck up and looked at me through the glass with twinkling diamond eyes.

'Flicker!' I shouted in delight. 'You came back!'

I flung open the window and leaned out to greet him, marvelling at how huge and mighty my once tiny friend had become. He was a beautiful deep ruby red and he glimmered as his scales rippled. His eyes shone brighter than any star. He beat his now enormous wings and rose up into the air, turning in circles as if to show off just how brilliant he had become.

'Wow!' I cried. 'Look at you!'

Coming back down to us, he brought his huge head closer and Lolli reached out to touch his scaly

nostril. He flickered gold and let out a puff of smoke that curled around her like a blanket.

Then he dipped his head lower, until his neck was touching the window ledge, right outside.

'Are you kidding?' I cried.

Lolli giggled and squeezed my arm and then gave me a little push towards Flicker.

I grinned at her and climbed up onto the windowsill. Carefully I swung one leg over Flicker's neck and hung on with both arms. The air was cold but I didn't feel it, not leaning against the warm glow of my dragon's body.

I'd dreamed about flying, and it might have felt pretty real at the time, but actually doing it is a whole other matter. I tell you, riding a dragon is just about as incredible as you could ever imagine it to be. And then times that like a gazillion trillion on top. Rising up into the air, I just couldn't stop laughing. Up, up, up . . .

And as we flew Flicker changed colour, from fiery red to azure blue, from crimson to blazing orange to deep purple, lime green, brilliant white and midnight black. All the colours of my dream. And I laughed again as I felt a rumble and a mighty jet of flame burst out of Flicker's mouth.

As we soared across the moonlit sky I saw something on the horizon. A dot. Not just one dot – five.

Five dots that grew bigger and bigger as they flapped their way towards us. And the next second I saw the sky lit up by the fiery breath of Sunny, Crystal, Dodger and Maxi. And then I heard Tinkle's song. It filled the air and it filled my head with images too: rivers of fire and ice, the flickering green of the Northern Lights and volcanoes erupting with colour – erupting with dragons!

I remembered what Jim had said about his wife, Molly. She had told him to let their son go and he would come back one day. Well, we had let the dragons go and here they were again. Maybe not to stay, but to visit.

Flying back over the rooftops, I saw Lolli, waving madly from the window. And in the streets beyond I spotted the houses where Ted, Kat, Kai and Liam would be. Asleep and dreaming of their dragons. But a dream – any dream – is just the beginning of an even greater story.

And as Flicker changed colour like a fiery kaleidoscope, I knew this was no dream. This was the real deal.

So, that's how it happened, how we ended up growing dragons, living with dragons and flying with dragons. And if, like me, you dream of dragons, then that's good. Because the world needs dragons. Sometimes you have to look for the magic, and I mean *really* look, under the brambles and in the nettly places at the very edges where most people never think to look. And you might have to dig and dig and dig until your arms ache from digging. Which is why you need to get yourself a superhero squad and someone to pop a caramel toffee or two your way – you know, the kind of people who are like the very best jam tarts – the ones that stick together.

Who knows, maybe one day, *you'll* find a dragon-fruit tree growing too.

And if you do, well, get ready for the ride of your life!

Andy Shepherd is a children's writer working on middle-grade fiction and picture books. She lives near Cambridge with her husband, two sons and their border collie. She spends her spare time trying to figure out how to move this beautiful city closer to the sea. *The Boy Who Flew with Dragons* is her third book. You can follow her on Twitter @andyjshepherd or Facebook https://www.facebook.com/andyjshepherd/

Sara Ogilvie is an award-winning artist/illustrator. She was born in Edinburgh in 1971 and lives in Newcastle upon Tyne. Sara's many picture books include *The Detective Dog* by Julia Donaldson, *The Worst Princess* by Anna Kemp, and *Izzy Gizmo* by Pip Jones. Her middle-grade fiction includes Phil Earle's *Demolition Dad* (and others in the Storey Street series).

www.saraogilvie.com

www.nbillustration.co.uk/sara-ogilvie

Acknowledgements

I've been lucky to have three opportunities to get my thanks in. Just as well really, because it's taken a long time to get published so the list of thank-yous has been pretty extensive!

So, to kick off part three, a massive thank-you to all the teachers and librarians who have taken the dragons into their hearts and their classes, schools and libraries. I can't thank you all enough for your enthusiasm and hard work getting the books into the hands of readers. My special thanks to Scott Evans (@thereaderteacher) for always giving the dragons such a brilliant shout-out.

Great teachers really are like superheroes. And I was lucky to have one of the best. David Cadwallader – my ace English teacher in secondary school, the one responsible for planting the idea that I could write in the first place. Even through the lean years of hardly writing anything, that deep-rooted belief stayed with me. David and his wife Linda are the kinds of teachers who make all the difference. So thank you!

Another huge thanks to the bonkersly brilliant Mellie Buse and Martin Franks, whose early encouragement gave me the confidence to go that extra mile and see if I could make this happen – and thank you for keeping me, if not sane, then suitably entertained along the way!

I'd like to thank Norberto Cuevas, Aura Cuevas and Arely Hernandez for helping me find out more about the magical dragon-fruit tree and sending me so many fantastic photos of it growing wild.

Thank you to my lovely agent Jo Williamson and my fabulous editors Georgia Murray and Talya Baker, for all their hard work and help, and for looking after me along the way.

A massive thank-you to Sara Ogilvie for all her gorgeous illustrations and eye-catching covers. They are simply a joy.

My love and thanks to Mum, Dad and Pete and all my wonderful family and friends – your endless support and cheering on means so much.

Ian, Ben and Jonas, these books are in the world because of you. Always remember, wherever you are, there is magic.

Piccadilly

P R E S S

Thank you for choosing a Piccadilly Press book.

If you would like to know more about our authors, our books or if you'd just like to know what we're up to, you can find us online.

www.piccadillypress.co.uk

You can also find us on:

We hope to see you soon!